The Kaleidoscope Man

Elizabeth Hopkinson

Elizabeth Hopkinson was found beneath a gooseberry bush at the bottom of a garden in Camden Town, London, in the early 1980s. When she finally managed to get out from under it she found herself in Shropshire. She was inspired to write her first novel, *The Mystery of the Ball*, at the age of eight, while staying at the home of celebrated crime writer Ruth Rendell. She has been writing regularly since the age of sixteen, and this is her first published novel.

The Kaleidoscope Man

Elizabeth Hopkinson

FireCrest
Fiction

The Kaleidoscope Man
An Original Publication of FireCrest Fiction
An imprint of FireCrest International Limited

First published in 2008 by FireCrest International Ltd
62 Stone Street Llandovery Carmarthenshire

Copyright © Elizabeth Hopkinson 2008

Elizabeth Hopkinson has asserted her moral right to be identified as the author of this book

Cover image: Maxim Kalmykoff
[http://kalmykoff.com]
Cover design: Mick Cathcart
Typography and typesetting by Peter Brookesmith and Lesley Riley

A CIP catalogue record for this book is available from the British Library

ISBN
978-1-906174-02-6

Printed and bound in the UK by Lightning Source UK Ltd, Milton Keynes,
and in the USA by Lightning Source Inc, LaVergne, Tennessee

CONDITIONS OF SALE
All rights reserved. No part of this publication may be reproduced, stored in
a retrieval system, or transmitted in any form or by any means, electronic, mechanical,
photocopying, recording or otherwise, without the prior permission of the publisher.

This book is sold subject to the condition that it shall not, by way of trade or otherwise, be
lent, re-sold, hired out or otherwise circulated without the publisher's prior consent in any form
of binding or cover other than the one in which it is published and without a similar condition
being imposed on the subsequent purchaser

*For my mother,
as ever,
with love*

Other echoes
Inhabit the garden. Shall we follow?
Quick, said the bird, find them, find them,
Round the corner. Through the first gate,
Into our first world, shall we follow
The deception of the thrush? Into our first world.
There they were, dignified, invisible,
Moving without pressure, over the dead leaves,
In the autumn heat, through the vibrant air,
And the bird called, in response to
The unheard music hidden in the shrubbery,
And the unseen eyebeam crossed, for the roses
Had the look of flowers that are looked at.
There they were as our guests, accepted and accepting.
So we moved, and they, in a formal pattern,
Along the empty alley, into the box circle,
To look down into the drained pool.
Dry the pool, dry concrete, brown edged,
And the pool was filled with water out of sunlight,
And the lotos rose, quietly, quietly,
The surface glittered out of heart of light,
And they were behind us, reflected in the pool.
Then a cloud passed, and the pool was empty.
Go, said the bird, for the leaves were full of children,
Hidden excitedly, containing laughter.
Go, go, go, said the bird: human kind
Cannot bear very much reality.

—T.S. Eliot, *Burnt Norton*

1

THE DOGS SWUNG SLOWLY. The breeze rotated their hardening bodies, mocking their stillness. The tree bent its bough and the man watching gazed dispassionately at what he had created.

His gaze flicked back to the house. The windows were still dark, unseeing. He shifted his weight slightly, allowed himself one more look at the house. And then moving silently, though there was no need now, he left. Still the dogs swung, and the tree bowed its head in grief.

IN THE HOUSE the mother stirred. Some elusive thought danced on the edge of her mind. She longed to wake and grasp it firmly, but she did not. Her mind put up its barricades and let itself drift. On the other side of the wall her daughter lay curled tightly in a ball. Her fingers laced the sheets as if they were reins and she were galloping far away. A dog ran beside her. She smiled in her dream.

THE GIRL WOKE. A new day. Though thinking it strange that her mother's door was still closed, signifying sleep, she shook the thought from her head. She walked downstairs and then outside.

HER SCREAMS woke the neighbours.

Fear encircled the small cottage, dragging the mother outside. So that her eyes too fell upon the stiffening bodies suspended from the tree.

The mother wrapped her arms around her baby and rocked her.

"I love him," whispered the mother, her eyes upon the dogs.

The girl said nothing. Together, they watched the neighbours, held up by sticks, as they crossed the lawn.

THE ELDERLY LADY stopped rigid. Her face crumpled. Her own dog weaved around her heels whining at her distress. The breaths tore ragged at her throat. She waved her husband back. He stopped irresolutely, torn between the desire to reach out and heal, and the knowledge that everything seen would not be forgotten. He turned, his feet leaving trails in the dew.

"No," said the neighbour. Her gnarled hand shook on her stick. The parrot's head bobbed, up, down, up, down.

The mother nodded.

"He sat at my table," said the neighbour. "He drank my tea, out of my cups." Her voice changed. It began to reach out, accuse and hurt. The mother let it. Nothing was unbroken now, there was no more left to hurt.

"He lay in my bed," said the mother.

"Out of your own choice. You took him freely, willingly, into your life." Her voice shook. The mother sighed.

"Yes. And you chose to summon him to your table."

"Only on approval." The hand on the parrot's head was rigid now. The girl watched the parrot.

"Maybe I was wrong." The mother stared at the neighbour.

"You should have known better." The neighbour turned and traversed the lawn. Her back tightly indignant.

The girl sat where she had been left. The crystal hung from the window frame. She watched the sunlight on it. She shut one eye and then the other. But she could not hold her head still and neither would the light be still. She shut her eyes.

HE SEEMED TO WALK under the tree. The screams echoed and the tree shook its branches.

"We're fine Granny, it is very sunny here."

The girl nodded, laughed obediently. He faded from her sight.

"No mummy's not here at the moment. Yes, I'll tell her you rang."

She put the phone down, looked at her mother and returned to her seat.

"How was Granny?"

"Fine, she says the garden is looking very beautiful."

The mother surveyed the girl. A fluttering of panic threatened to overwhelm her. It became crashing waves. White horses reared, dragging at her. The water slopped into her mouth, but her head would not rise, and the water filled her mouth, and the salt stung.

"Mummy?" The girl's serenity flickered, the child emerged briefly, before unseen hands pushed it away and the curtains closed.

"Drink this."

Tea. Hot and a syrup in the bottom, because he never liked his sugar stirred. The mother gulped and the liquid burned, the pain bringing her back into balance. The walls regained their rightful places and the sky hung where it should.

"Why," she asked as she knew she should, "why did you not tell Granny?"

The girl traced the grain of the table with her fingernail.

"I couldn't find the words."

"No," agreed the mother.

"I don't," murmured the girl, as if discussing some finer grammatical point, "think there are the words."

"No," agreed the mother, who had lost all hers. She looked at the clock. It was lunchtime.

"It's lunchtime," she said.

The girl did not answer. How can the day be structured, when the world is not. When time has no sense, where does lunch belong in that aftermath?

"I think a little soup," said the mother, clinging to her structure.

THE PROBLEM WITH THE SOUP, thought the girl, as she chased endless strands of spaghetti round her bowl, was not the soup itself, but him. The soup was his soup. Even the smell as it rose became solid and formed a person, who leant over her mother, arms around hers, fingers tangled in her hair. The girl dropped her spoon. It fell heavily and displaced the soup. The soup trickled along the table top and dripped onto the floor. And there were no dogs to lick it up.

THE CLOCKS no longer bore any relation to time, had no pity on the mind. They stayed stationary, as did the sun, shining. The thought of the elderly neighbours' roasting joint made a mockery of their tinned soup. And Sunday had no right to be.

THEY PLAYED CARDS, since actions can ward off thought. The phone rang, indecently loud in the silence. The peals went on and the receiver throbbed. The girl's voice filled the room as the answering machine clicked in. The mother could not relate the giggling message to the still presence beside her.

THE BOLTS, STIFF FROM DISUSE, grumbled. The mother hunted frantically for keys. Once the house was suitably barricaded, she rushed upstairs, the darkness below making her stumble. The girl was sleeping fully clothed. She lay tightly circled round herself, as if by holding herself together she could remain whole.

THE MOTHER'S SHEETS, not changed since before the row, smelt of him. As she pulled back the duvet, his scent filled her nostrils, catching her throat. Longing rose up. She forced it down. She climbed under the duvet. His smell rose from its folds. She could not sleep.

She counted sheep. But they mutated into him. She recited poems learned in the schoolroom but the sounds warped until his voice spoke through her lips. She shook her head as if the physical could cast out the mental. She gave in. He rose up before and overcame her. She sat all night, the curls of cigarette smoke seeming to outline his presence beside her. By the morning he seemed as solid as if he had never gone. She drew back the curtains. The sun shone. The bed was empty. Only smoke hung in the room. She pushed open the window, and the smell of morning and the songs of birds entered the room. She dressed, neatly, carefully.

NEXT DOOR her daughter lay flat on her back, her arms tight by her side. Her long thick hair fanned around her head. The heaviness of her hair made her features seem even more delicate. A small slender nose stretching to a full mouth as if breaking into adulthood. Her face screwed up as if she could hold out the world. The sunlight touched her face as it slipped past the open curtains and filled the small room. But this did not make her smile. She could hear the shuffle of her mother dressing through the wall. She shut her eyes tighter. The door creaked. She felt the slight breeze from the loose window on the landing. She heard her mother sigh.

"Morning Laura, time to get up."

Laura did not move. She heard the click as her mother turned on the main light hoping to drive her up and out of bed.

"Laura, I know you're awake." Her mother's voice was tighter now. Laura waited. She knew what came next.

"Actually I don't care. Stay in bed." The door slammed, shocking her. She heard her mother's feet on the stairs and then the cottage fell silent.

Laura sat up. Her hair hung down her back, curly. She frowned. Confused. The ritual of the morning broken. They rowed every morning, she and her mother, about school. A meaningless yet essential part of the framework of her day. The routine had soothed Laura through her parents' divorce, through Kevin's disappearance. She had felt that all could change, all but that routine. But now it had. Laura swung her feet out of the bed and padded across the old wooden floorboards to the window. She curled herself onto the window ledge, her tall frame filling the space, making her aware of her own growing body. The garden was sunny. Bright flowers grew near the house before giving way to a gently sloping lawn and the tree. Laura's tree. She felt her stomach heave and bile flood her mouth. From the window she could see the raw earth. Three mounds. Three small crooked crosses. Longing suddenly for maternal comfort, she ran down the stairs.

IN THE KITCHEN Alison mindlessly unloaded the dishwasher. The shock of yesterday had given way to a blankness. A greyness washed through her. She put the saucepan in the fridge and turned the kettle on. Her face though beautiful was lined. She looked at herself in the small mirror that hung by the back door. She traced the lines with her fingers. Divorce, Laura, Kevin, Mother. Could she name every line? Kevin. She rested her head on the back door. The glass was cold on her skin. Kevin. His arms encircling her. Safe. She'd laughed. What at, she did not know. It didn't matter. She gasped as pain flashed through her. His smile. She hugged herself, holding herself as the pain bashed against her ribs. She had not known mental anguish could cause such real physical pain. Still slim, she thought bitterly, as her hands encircled her waist as his hands had done. Slim and single. She turned roughly away as the kettle shrieked indignantly. Her freckled hand shook slightly as she poured hot water on the coffee granules and the water missed the mug and splashed on the sideboard, biting her hand. She shook it and turned quickly. But the dogs weren't there and their biscuit box was still on the side. She picked it up and held it. She drew out three biscuits and fingered them. The hall door slammed and Laura appeared in the kitchen. She slipped the biscuits in her pocket. They felt comforting there.

LAURA WALKED FORWARD. Alison waited warily for some snide comment, a scathing remark. But Laura hung her head. Alison hugged her and once again Laura became her little child.

He had loved Laura: called her beautiful, precious. Been kinder to her than her own father. Hard to love another man's child.

"Mum, do I have to go to school?" Hard to love one's own.

"Yes." Alison pushed her away. The closeness scaring her. Aware she could no longer protect and shield her daughter from the world. Could not cope with another person's pain, barely keeping upright under her own. "I have to go to work and I can't leave you here on your own."

"I'll be fine."

"Laura!"

"Fine." She turned away, her slouching teenage back fending off the world.

ALISON LEFT HER AT THE BUS STOP. Laura did not say goodbye. Alison drove slowly to the town where she worked as a secretary for a solicitor. The car smelt of dogs from the previous weekend. The smell was poignant, sensual as any memory. The lakes, the three of them. The dogs. He'd laughed when she was tired and slung her on his shoulder. Carrying her squawking till he had dropped her in the bracken by her daughter, and the dogs had bounced round slobbering, their tails wagging. Joyously alive. Alive.

"Morning Alison," said Jo, the receptionist. Her skirt was very short. She wore a lot of make-up and on her neck were three red love bites. Alison turned away and trailed upstairs. Mr Peter Rogers was on the phone, shouting at someone. She switched her computer on. It chugged into life. The screensaver came up. She'd forgotten. The dogs. She winced. Their bodies swung. So heavy to cut down from the apple tree, the knife rubbing fruitlessly against the taut rope. And such deep holes to dig. She typed automatically. Her eyes blurred with tears. She did not see the screen, nor register the content. Time passed.

When Peter Rogers came in a while later he found her sitting at her desk holding three dog biscuits and weeping.

LAURA GOT OFF THE BUS. The school gates hung drunkenly open.

"What's up *your* nose?" asked Barney, his ginger hair spiked up, shining. The same colour as Red's coat.

"Go away," she pushed him roughly.

"Hey lanky, watch who you shove," he said, pushing her back.

"Leave me alone!" she snapped.

"Fine." He walked away.

Her friends rushed up, giggling.

"Barney fancies you."

I would have cared, she thought. She swung her bag over her shoulder and crossed the yard.

"She's embarrassed!" screamed Harriet, chasing after her.

"Laura fancies Barney," they chanted. The words swam round her, enfolding her. They became glass and the glass blocked her in and then there was nothing, only their mouths opening and closing, but no sound. She closed her eyes, but then the dogs swung and the sight of her friends' mindless faces was better. In her box she could not hear them.

She found herself in the chemistry lab. The board was covered with numbers and letters. The teacher spoke, she watched his mouth move and his hands gesture. His jaws reminded her of a barking dog. She felt an elbow in her side. The box shattered and noise flooded in, drowning her.

"Have you done your homework, Lol?"

She shook her head.

"Lol! You said I could copy. I'm going to get in trouble now. It's all your fault!"

My fault. Is it my fault? Why, why, and they swung in her head. And she could not rebuild her box. And now she could hear the creaking of the rope and see the flecks of spittle from their desperate attempts to breathe, and she could see the patches of flattened grass where he had stood and hauled their bodies up and they had made no sound. And their bodies surrounded her now, and someone was screaming.

IN THE OFFICE of Rogers and James, Solicitors and Commissioners for Oaths, the phone rang.

"Good morning," said Jo, "how can I help? Alison Mannings, certainly, please hold the line."

Upstairs the extension buzzed. Peter Rogers rubbed Alison's back reluctantly, unsure what he should do with this gently sobbing lady. He picked up the phone, grateful for the distraction.

"What? Oh. I'll tell her."

Downstairs Jo began to file her nails. She held them out in front of her and smiled her spoilt smile. Silly Alison, she thought, not holding onto that sexy Kevin, let herself go, didn't she. Her and that sulky daughter of hers. How funny. Did this pink really suit her? She frowned and placed her hand on her thigh. Maybe a slightly darker tone would be better.

"Alison, that was the school. Laura passed out in class. They want you to go and pick her up."

"But I can't, I must work. I must work." She gestured with the dog biscuit at the screen.

"It's okay," he said soothingly. "I'll take you."

She followed him downstairs, incapable of thought.

"Jo, I'm just popping out for a bit."

"No probs Mr R." She gave him a flashing smile.

"I do wish she wouldn't call me that," said Peter Rogers as he led Alison to his car.

He drove very fast, like Kevin. The countryside flickered by. Kevin had loved cars, fast ones, flashy ones. Jason hadn't been a car fan.

LAURA WAS SITTING VERY STILL in sickbay. The television was on with the sound turned down and on the screen a man shouted at a woman.

"There you are, dear," said the matron. "Your parents have come to take you home."

Laura looked up. Her skin felt loose round her face as if her bones had shrunk inside her. Her mother was holding a dog biscuit and the man looked as if he wished he were not there.

"Have a few days off," said Peter Rogers as he deposited them by their car. "You're both in shock. A few days' rest will do you the power of good." He smiled hopefully at them. Laura watched his lips move. "One thing though," he turned back towards Alison. "Why did he do it?"

2

ACROSS THE OTHER SIDE OF TOWN from the solicitors where Alison worked was a row of old Georgian houses. Inside number five, Frank Hargreaves sat in his office. The tall walls were lined with books. Not well-mannered wall-dressing books, but real grubby, well-thumbed books that hung off the shelves or retreated backwards as if ashamed of their own frivolity. Fantasy sat uneasily by war poetry. Modern fiction lay entwined with classics. Dotted among the books were photos. His parents. His daughter. His racehorse. His wife. Fanning out around him across the floor lay paperwork. He plucked at random and a phone bill appeared. The figures, demanding in bold type, caught his eye, and he frowned.

"Annie!" A girl appeared through the doorway. A tall girl wearing a dressing gown that was too small, so that her arms shot out the ends revealing slender wrists and dainty hands. She leant against the doorframe, a bundle of tissue in her hand.

"What?"

Frank regarded his daughter.

"Why is the phone bill quite so extortionate?"

The girl looked into the room, her eyes wandered past him and rested on the bookcase.

"Ringing mum," she said.

Frank pushed his hair back from where it flopped untidily across his forehead, giving him an air of diffidence or laziness. His eyes were cold blue and were now resting on his daughter. He waited. Gradually a spot of red appeared on each cheekbone and began to spread.

"I'm sorry," said the girl hanging her head. She sneezed and groaned.

"Your mother is in France. The numbers that seem to have racked up rather a large bill are local."

"Sorry. Dad I feel really ill."

"Go and lie down then. Why are you wandering round if you feel ill?" He flapped his hand and the phone bill fluttered to the ground.

Sighing, but feeling too ill to point out to her father that he had summoned her, Annie turned round and trailed back to her nest on the sofa. She flicked the remote at the television and the stationary figures jumped back to life and resumed their story. Frank returned to his paperwork. He came across a thankyou card from a client he had forgotten about. Mrs Philips. Musing on Mrs Philips, he wandered away from his office into the large kitchen. He opened the fridge. An old tomato sat on the shelf surrounded by half-eaten pots of yoghurt and a few cans of lager. Closing the fridge door he discovered the milk by the kettle and poured himself a mug of coffee from the pot. He returned to his office, the card still in his hand. Mrs Philips. He found her file and the accompanying press cutting. A beaming picture of Detective Sergeant Trent loomed out of the paper, smugness trailed across his brow.

"What a horrible man." Frank drew a moustache across the upper lip and then a pair of spectacles. He groaned at his own childish behaviour and then, yawning, returned the cutting to the file and dropped it onto the floor. He rested his chin on his hands as he peered out of the window. Mrs Jones passed, her dog pulling her, intent on reaching the park. Frank picked up the photo on the desk. His wife Kate smiled back at him. He ran his finger down the freckles that speckled her nose. Sighing he carefully put the photo back down and picked up her last letter.

I feel a real sense of peace here. A sense of coming to know myself.

Frank missed her.

ON THE OUTSKIRTS of the village, a few miles from the town where Frank sat, Alison turned the car into the small driveway behind the cottage. The late summer roses were fading now, their delicate petals curling up, preparing for winter and sleep. Alison glanced at her daughter. Laura's eyes were firmly closed. Her face in sleep was relaxed, sweet, the scowls of adolescence gone. Alison stopped the car and cut the engine. Laura stirred and woke, her face closing down as the first glow of consciousness pervaded her mind.

The silence in the house was overwhelming. It hung syrup-like from the low beams, crept into every murky corner and mocked them. Laura trailed upstairs. Alison heard her feet drag along the floorboards, then the creak and groan of the bed as Laura flopped into it. Then only silence. Alison sat down at the kitchen table. She lit a cigarette and wished she were still at work. At least there she could lose herself in some subtlety of law. Escape. Not sit here within these four walls so laden with memories that they threatened to spill over and drown her. She lit a second cigarette, concentrating on the lighter, the colour of the flame, the burning tip, the smoke filling her lungs and making her head spin. But as her head spun, so Peter Rogers' last words surfaced and began to parade. Wherever she looked she saw only the word 'why?'

She fought against her curiosity. She switched on the kettle, made coffee, tidied the kitchen, scrubbed the sink and then the cooker, but her mind would not come clean and still the word marked everything. Something inside her shied away. Perhaps instinct, perhaps fear. But was blankness better than knowledge? Could the truth really set you free, or was it better simply to forget? But can I walk away and be truly free if I do not know why? Or will it haunt me, follow me, whispering in my ear when I stand in a shop or on a beach, or when I lie in some half-sleep in the grey lands? I don't know.

No. I must know. Sand can't cover my head forever, I can't always look the other way. I can't exist in that grey state where the question will haunt me. I must know. For only then can I be truly free. Only then can I understand, and perhaps some day forgive, and then life need not be lost but can bring me hope.

But the fear flooded up. Fighting it now, she pulled the cooker away from the wall and began to scrub the paintwork behind it.

A corner of paper protruded from under the grimy base of the cooker. She sat back on her heels and pulled it out. It was a photo. A photo of her, Kevin, Laura and the dogs. The dogs sat clustered round his feet. Their eyes gazed adoringly up at him. Their dad. And now the 'why' hit her. How could he have done it? His leaving she could cope with, but the dogs, that was different, that was unbelievable. She had to know.

IN FRANK'S OFFICE the phone rang. The noise drew him from his own reflections. He picked it up.

"Frank Hargreaves speaking."

Alison looked at the phone. She paused. The voice sounded so capable, so assured, self contained. She felt herself tremble as if struck.

"Hello?" said Frank. "Hello?"

"Hello," replied Alison doubtfully.

"Can I help you?"

"I don't know." She wound the cord around her finger. He had always done that. On the blower, he had called it. She felt burning on the rims of her eyes again. Her sight blurred.

"If you can tell me what's the matter, I may be able to help." His voice was soft, patient.

She tried to form a sentence, but the words whirled out of reach and far away and she could not grasp them.

"Why?" she asked. The only word she could see.

"Why what?" he replied, still patient.

She looked out the window. The tree seemed smaller, as if shameful of its own role. "My dogs," she said.

"Your dogs?" Frank looked at the phone. The voice of the nameless lady was well spoken, well educated. Sweet even. But there was no sense in her words. He felt her unravelling.

"Why did he do it?" she asked him and then again, her tone rising now, "Why?"

"Shall I come and see you?" he asked.

SHE WAITED IN THE LIMBO that absence of choice can bring. The energy required to pick up the phone, to decide to pick up the phone, that brief touch with the outside world had rendered her shattered and cold. She saw clearly that she had to know why, but the final step seemed too big to make. She could not change his coming, but she could change the next step. Quietly she made her way upstairs, remembering to avoid the fourth step, the one that had always creaked. Still creaking, he had said, every morning on his way downstairs. And she had laughed every time. Perhaps it was not the loneliness that got you in the end, but the small actions that you missed. A whole person, a whole world built out of minute everyday happenings.

She pushed open Laura's door. Laura lay curled up, still wearing her school uniform. Her breathing was deep. Her school shirt stretched over her growing breasts. She needs new shirts, thought Alison inconsequentially. Softly she closed the door and returned downstairs. Would not knowledge bring her daughter peace? Laura hated secrets, always had. Had screamed as a small child when told something was a secret. Had loved Kevin because he had not excluded her as Jason had. Jason had liked secrets. He had treasured them, held them close to his chest and smiled because you did not know his secrets. She was well shot of *him* at any rate.

Wheels scrunched on the gravel. Alison started. She rushed to the door, perhaps it was him, perhaps he had come back, with arms full of roses. On their first anniversary she had come home and the house had been full. Petals had layered the carpets and had made a path up the stairs, along the landing and into the bedroom. And there he had been lying. Naked in a bed of petals. A Hollywood fantasy. She swallowed. Lust churned inside her. Smooth, broad shoulders. Strong, toned and brown, and a chest to fold into. Arms to hold you, hug you, protect you. *I'll always protect you,* he had said.

She opened the door. A tall man stood on the doorstep, thin to the point of lankiness. His hair flopped over his forehead and his eyes were blue.

"Frank Hargreaves," said the man, extending his hand. She took it. It was warm and firm. Reassuring like his voice. "You must be Alison."

"Yes," said Alison, doubting her own name. "I must be."

He watched her as she made coffee. Her face was open, intelligent, naive even, he thought.

Her hand shook slightly as she placed the mug on the pine table. The coffee spilt and trickled slowly down the side of the mug. Frank rubbed it into the table and watched as it faded slowly away. She sat hunched over her mug, her fingers laced together round the patterned china, her rings glinting in the sunshine. They sat in silence. Alison fought with her mind, trying to get a hold on words that would send him away.

He watched her fighting and waited. She saw his eyes upon her and looked away, but her gaze landed on the tree and she was forced to look back into his blue eyes. Kevin's eyes had been blue. She looked at the table, at his long, thin fingers, where other hands had lain. Other hands that had picked hers up and kissed her knuckles and other lips that had called her 'My girl'. She rubbed her eyes and looked straight up at him. She had to know.

"The dogs," she said.

He jumped.

"What happened to the dogs?" he asked. The pain flickered in her eyes.

"He hanged them," she said.

Frank recoiled.

"I'm sure there is a good reason." Even as she saw the faint trace of scorn scurry across his eyes, she knew her words to be false.

"Who?" asked Frank, pushing images to one side, maintaining clear detachment.

"My partner. Kevin Todd."

"Partner?" he queried, sensing the hesitation over the description.

"Well he was, he left, a week ago."

The empty house. Monday evening, take-away evening. Laden with bags of food she had banged the door, calling his name. The dogs had rushed forward, snuffling in delight at the bags. She had pushed them roughly away. If she had known she would have held them close, never let them go. Stillness in the house. An emptiness. His boots not by the door. Neither pair. Upstairs. The wardrobe open. The door hanging forlornly. The shelves empty. Gone.

"Why did he leave?" asked Frank, watching emotions scroll across her face.

"I don't know," she said. "We were happy."

The bafflement struck him. A bewildered child, stumbling in distress.

"Are you sure?" he asked.

"Yes!" she snapped, turning on him. Anger from pain.

"Okay," he soothed her. Patting the air with his hand. The motion calmed her. "I understand this is very difficult for you."

"He just left." She spoke as if to herself. "Left. There was no sign of him. No trace, as if he had never been here. As if I had dreamt the whole thing."

"Did you call him?"

She nodded. Her face tight with the memory. Fingers scrabbling on the phone. His voice hard, different. Her screams. Weeping anguish.

"He told me not to try to find him."

"Were you tempted?"

She looked at him and nodded.

"But you didn't?"

She shook her head, but he watched her eyes and saw the humiliation behind them. Crawling the streets at night searching for his car. The tears wet on her cheeks. And when she returned overwrought the dogs had comforted her, crowding round her, loving her.

So she had tried, but had failed.

"And you still have no idea why he left."

"No," she said, but something glimmered, a thought, a sound. "I think a girl giggled in the background."

"Was there someone else?"

"How do I know?" she pleaded. "I thought I knew him. But this." Her arm gestured to the tree.

"Do you know it was him? The dogs, I mean." Frank watched her. His eyes narrowed. Vengeance is a terrible thing.

"They would have barked. They trusted him. They would have gone silently with him." She stood up roughly and turned away, retching over the sink.

"You're sure?"

She looked up at him and frowned. Still leaning over the sink, she looked away, blankly, across the garden.

"I heard Laura scream. I ran out and I knew. I just knew it had been him. I dreamt, I think," she paused. "It's hazy but I dreamt I heard him in the night and then I saw them and..." She ground to a stop.

"Who's Laura?"

"My daughter."

Frank thought of Annie.

"Where is she?"

"Upstairs." Alison inclined her head upwards. "Asleep."

"Does she know why he left?" asked Frank.

Alison flinched.

"She said I must have nagged him too much." Her voice was hard. Laura's flint-like face stabbed at her brain. Her laugh humourless. *Oh well done Mum, chased another one away.*

"She was so sweet when she was little. Lovely smiling little girl. Now..." She shook her head.

"How old is she?"

"Fourteen."

"Horrible age," said Frank. "She'll grow out of it. Don't worry."

"She was fine with Kevin," continued Alison. "She liked him. It was just me."

"You're her mother. Was she upset when he left?" he asked, the blue eyes sharpening.

"I don't know," said Alison. "We don't talk much, really. Perhaps she blamed me, maybe it was easier for her to be angry than sad."

"It often is at that age," agreed Frank. "But they got on well?"

She nodded.

"They never argued?"

"Only about shoes," replied Alison. She smiled into the past. Frank frowned.

"When we were still speaking she said he was like her brother, father, best friend rolled into one, and then he did that to her. Why did he do it?" The question emerged again, becoming more pressing now. "To me, maybe I'd done something, I don't know. But she loved those dogs. Why hurt her?"

"I don't know," said Frank.

Her eyes strayed outside again. She got up. He followed her. The air had a hint of winter. A slight chill warning of what was on the way. She showed him the tree and the graves they had dug, the small crosses already crooked as if he had reached out and touched them, ruined them.

She looked at her watch, but the time had no meaning.

"Walk with me," she said.

THE WOOD WAS DAMP. The leaves on the ground gave a muffled rustle as their feet padded along. Side by side he could not see her face. He sensed her relax, movement bringing relief. She paused briefly by a tree but did not speak. She remembered the feel of the bark against her back, his breath on her neck, harsh. No: not harsh, gentle, kind. Why did she remember it as harsh? She walked forwards away from the tree.

"How did you meet him?" asked Frank, his eyes sliding sideways to watch her.

"I'd just got divorced. We had to sell the house, move to the town. I hate towns." She kicked a stone. The pain made her gasp, her blood warmed for a moment. "My pipes burst. He came home with me and never left. We danced."

"Danced?"

"Life felt so light. Have you ever felt like that?" She looked at him, her eyes intense.

"Yes," he said thinking of Kate in the sunshine. "But it's not real."

"What do you mean not real?" As if he were twisting her memories.

"It is an illusion, it passes. Maybe it flashes back for an hour or maybe even a minute, but it isn't permanent."

"But it was," she said, staring at him. "It was."

"Fine," he shrugged his shoulders and hunched his hands deeper into pockets. But his eyes were narrow.

"WHAT DID HE DO for a living?" asked Frank later as they sat warming themselves in the kitchen.

"This and that. Odd jobs." She averted her eyes.

"Nothing," said a scornful voice.

They looked up. Laura stood in the doorway leaning against the frame. Frank was reminded sharply of Annie earlier in that exact same pose. But this girl was scowling at him. Her face tight and closed. Enveloped in three jumpers, still in her short school skirt, long legs.

"Laura," said Alison flushing slightly. "This is Frank. Frank Hargreaves."

"Found yourself a new man already have you? Quick work Mum, quick work." She stamped across the kitchen to the drinks cupboard. She poured herself a whiskey. Alison did not bother to reprimand her.

Bravado, thought Frank.

"Gonna support him like you did the last one?" She gulped the whiskey. Frank noticed a trace of a grimace cross her face.

"I didn't support him," said Alison.

Frank's blue eyes rested on her. She looked away. "Maybe a little. But his work was inconsistent." Frank watched her scrabble with her dignity. "Anyway Frank is going to find out why Kevin..." She flapped her hand. Laura shrugged. Frank watched her, noting the defensive curl of her shoulders, the smouldering face. She could not quite disguise the soft prettiness of her features.

"Did you like him?" asked Frank looking at Laura.

She pulled herself up onto the worktop and swung her legs.

"He was okay."

"You said you liked him," said Alison, turning appealingly to her daughter.

"Did I?" she said looking away.

"Yes," said Alison, "you did."

"You only hear what you want to hear Mum. Or see what you want to see." Laura jumped off the worktop. They heard her feet clumping on the stairs.

"I'm sorry about that," said Alison.

"Don't be."

Alison fiddled with her rings. Frank watched her twisting each one in turn. A strangely primitive action, as if warding off evil spirits.

"What do you want?" asked Frank. He leant forwards.

She glanced up, her eyes slipping away from his, unable to hold such intensity.

"Him," she murmured. His arms felt so solid round her, she lifted her hand to stroke his arm, but there was only empty air and her fingers hovered in distress.

"Really?" asked Frank, leaning forwards. "After what he did?" Pushing her now.

She put her hand against her cheek. Flesh on flesh. But it was not his hand. His hands had pulled the rope, tugged their bodies upwards. His hands had secured the rope. His hands had hanged them. She dropped her hand to the table.

"I don't know." The words were a plea. "I can't think, I can't decide. Do I have to?" She looked at him. Her soft brown eyes beseeched him to choose for her, to decide.

"You have a choice," he said, reluctant to make it for her. "Either you can forget and never know or wake in the night and wonder. Or you can know and draw a line. Resolve the past. But it must be your choice."

She hung her head. In her mind he laughed, his face thrown back, his mouth wide open. It would take over, she suddenly saw. Expand, overwhelm her. She could not be free, the dogs would still swing, if she did not know.

"I want to know why he did it."

Frank smiled at her. He softly licked his lips. A curiously touching motion. "Right," he said. She sensed a new tone in his voice, a ring of triumph, of anticipation. His spine seemed to stretch and he sat taller. The traces of diffidence gone from his body.

"What was he like?" asked Frank. "How would you describe him?"

She put her hand in her pocket and drew out the photo she had found. Reluctantly she handed it to him. He hadn't liked having his photo taken. Like people who believed it stole a piece of your soul. Frank looked at the picture. Kevin Todd smiled out. The mother and daughter seemed to crowd round him like the dogs, in adoration. He sat dominant above them. Frank shivered. He examined the man's features. His hair was very blond, slightly too long as if clinging to some long-gone era. His eyes were a striking blue, like a child's. Whether from just a trick of the light, or some photographic effect, they seemed oddly blank. His bone structure was clear and strong, the lines of the jaw and cheekbones long and sloping. Frank tucked the photo into his notepad.

"He's very handsome."

"Yes," she said eagerly. He saw her eyes wander to the photo, her fingers itch to hold it. He pulled the pad towards him.

"But what was he like in himself?"

She frowned, as if she had never considered it.

"Funny," she said slowly, searching for words. "Engaging." He had held her as they'd danced. Slowly the other dancers had slipped away and the walls fragmented. The music grew until they were all alone, the music replacing their blood. Their eyes fixed on one another, holding one another. "He made you feel like you were the only person in the world."

"Isolated?"

"No," she snapped turning on him. "He was all you needed, all you wanted." She smiled. He watched her eyes wander into the past.

"Do you have many friends?" he asked. His pen skittered on the paper.

"Yes, lots." Some tightness crept into her voice. Frank moved on.

"Where did he come from?"

"Nottingham, I think."

"You've met his family?"

"No, they died when he was a teenager."

"How sad," said Frank. A row of question marks spread along the page.

"Did he have many friends? People I could talk to, perhaps?"

"Yes," she said, but a confusion clouded her eyes.

"Names?" asked Frank gently.

His gentleness confused her further. Names swum away from her, she swallowed.

"Billy?" she ventured. "He got married."

"Any others?"

"The man with the garage. Old cars. Things like that. I can't remember his name."

"Where's the garage?" Frank lolled back in his chair, fighting the urge to interrogate.

"Marsden I think."

She looked hunted now. Her eyes were darting and her lips drying. He felt her breath shorten. Frank homed in.

"Do you know much about his past?" He spoke lightly, but a hard edge slithered through.

"He didn't talk about it!" She glared at him.

"Okay," he said. He watched her crumple downwards. "Don't worry, it'll be okay." He patted her hand. Like a soothing doctor, he calmed her, comforted her, held her.

Frank became aware of the lengthening shadows. He thought of Annie alone in the big house and felt a stab of anxiety, of panic. He breathed. It passed, washed away. He looked at Alison. She was staring out of the window.

"I must go," he said.

"Must you?" she asked, looking up as he stood. He placed one warm hand upon her shoulder and let it rest there for a moment. He squeezed it.

"It'll be okay," he said again, and left.

She could feel the imprint from his hand as she heard the car pull away down the lane. Could feel the warmth where his hand had rested. Did Kevin ever rest his hand like that? Had he ever? She could not think. She couldn't remember. His face flickered before her eyes. She poured herself a whiskey. Her fingers looked old. She tried to picture him again, screwing her eyes up. But he was breaking up, like an old film. The images crackled and the crackle turned into a laugh, his laugh. The sound echoed through her mind and would not stop.

3

AS HE LET THE HEAVY DOOR SLAM behind him, Frank called: "Annie?" The slam drifted through the house making it seem somehow quieter. Her name sounded too small in the large hallway. He flipped on the hall lights. A faint buzz came from the sitting room. He hurried down the corridor, feeling his heart thump against his chest. He pushed opened the door. Annie lay fast asleep curled in a ball on the sofa. Her mouth hung slightly open. The television glowed in the dimness, its sound turned down. Frank switched on the lamps and looked down at his sleeping daughter. He rocked her softly.

"Annie?"

She groaned and then her eyes opened sleepily.

"How are you darling?" he asked, surprised at the tenderness in his own voice.

She screwed her face up, trying to drive out sleep.

"Fine, thanks, Dad." She yawned.

"Would you like anything? Coffee? Food?"

"Coffee, please."

The kitchen too was in darkness. He boiled the kettle, staring out of the window at the gloom. Pouring water on coffee granules, he returned to the sitting room. Annie had sat up and changed the channel. New characters now wandered across the screen, some domestic argument ensued.

"Here you are."

"Thanks."

They sat side by side, half watching the television, in affectionate silence.

"Mum rang," said Annie as she began to wake up.

"How was she?" asked Frank, disappointed to have missed her.

"She sounded good. Asked where you were. I said you'd gone to see a man about a dog."

Frank laughed. Their old joke whenever anyone asked where he was. Annie giggled. Frank looked at his daughter with pride, glad to have her and not that sulky daughter of Alison's with her clump clump boots and that scowling face.

"What are those clump clump boots?" he asked idly.

"What Dad?" Annie looked at him.

"Clump clump boots."

"What are clump clump boots?"

"I don't know, that's why I'm asking you."

Annie giggled.

"Do you mean boots that go clump clump when you walk?"

Frank beamed.

"Precisely."

"You are funny. They're Doc Martens. Very fashionable at the moment. Why, who had them?"

"Daughter of this woman I went to see."

"The one about the dog?" Annie giggled at her own joke. But Frank did not. His face closed.

"What Dad?" Annie looked at him. Frank made a steeple with his fingers. He remembered making it for Annie when she was little, and her gurgling delight. Frank shook his head.

"Dad?" asked Annie again.

"I used to talk to your mother about cases. But..."

"Talk to me."

"I shouldn't," he said.

"Why not?"

"You're too," he stopped short on the final word.

"Young?" she said grinning. "Tell me."

"It's not nice."

"I can help." She turned her face towards him, enthusiastic and trusting. Adult, he thought suddenly. He wanted to wrap her in her duvet and tuck her up in bed. He didn't want her to grow up, to send her out into a world where people were evil and where evil things happened to innocent people. Didn't want her to meet a man like Kevin Todd. But perhaps she wouldn't. Perhaps she'd know. He drew the photo out of his notepad and handed it to her.

"What do you think of him?" He pointed at the man.

Annie took the photo and leant back into the sofa. He watched her frown, watched the tip of her tongue protrude between her lips with the effort of concentration.

"His eyes look blank," she said. "Good-looking but shuttered." She handed the photo back to him shaking her head.

"Have you ever seen him?" asked Frank.

"No," said Annie, her eyes flicking back to the television. There was silence for a moment. She looked back at her father.

"What's he done?" she asked.

"Nothing," said Frank.

"Dad!"

But he shook his head and getting up off the sofa, padded out of the sitting room. Annie turned back to the television, losing herself in the bright figures and their problems.

Frank leant his palms on the table and bounced on the balls of his feet, feeling the pull up through the tendons of his wrist. Blank, she had said, shuttered. A man without a past, without a family, a man who disappeared without a word, a man who had hanged three dogs. But why? He pulled out the photo again and examined it. His fury for such a wanton act made him shake. But overriding that was desire, the desire to understand.

He returned to the sitting room.

"Do you want something to eat?"

"Whatever," replied Annie sulkily.

"Annie," he said crossing the floor. "I don't want you to know. I want you to believe that people are good and nice and kind. I want to protect you. Keep you safe."

"I know," she said, eyes still on the screen.

"But perhaps I'm wrong." He waited. She looked up at him and surprised him with a smile.

"You are sweet Dad."

HE TOLD HER OVER SUPPER. He watched the horror and distress upon her face and wondered if he were doing the right thing, wished he knew. Why, he asked Kate silently, why go to France to find yourself, why not here, with me, with us? But even as he watched, he saw himself reflected in his daughter's eyes.

"But why did he do it?" she asked.

Frank smiled softly. "That's my girl," he said.

AFTER THEY HAD WATCHED A TRASHY FILM together in companionable outrage at the appalling acting, Frank packed his daughter off to bed and returned to his small office. The street outside was quiet, the lamps cast soft pools of light onto the pavement, far away a car backfired. He drew the curtains and turned on the lamps, filling the room with soft warm lighting. He poured himself a drink and began to pace. Toying with ideas as they rose, stopping to study the photo, staring into Kevin's eyes, noting the laughter lines round his mouth and the grooves stretching up the centre of his forehead. How can I know you? Or, indeed, *can* I know you? Who are you and what are you? Frank pinned the photo to the bookcase and stepped back, as if evaluating a great master. But the photo told him nothing, only what he already knew: that Alison and indeed Laura had adored him. Their bodies craning towards him, craving closeness, their faces upturned, their eyes alight.

Blind. Where had that word come from? Why blind? What had she said? *You only see what you want to see Mum.*

What if, mused Frank, you turned that statement round? What if you only saw what *he* wanted you to see? Perhaps.

The phone rang, the noise making him start. Reluctantly he dragged himself away.

It was his mother. Tipsy, he could hear it in her voice, that subtle slurring of the words, balancing on the edge of outright drunkenness. He let the waffle pass across him, knowing she would sooner or later get to the point. She did.

"Lucinda thinks her husband's having an affair," hissed his mother. Lucinda was his mother's next-door neighbour and, as she and her husband were both about eighty and devoted to one another, Frank considered this affair unlikely.

"Why?" he asked.

"Because she's not good enough for him!" His mother's voice rose rapidly.

"No, no, not that why. Why does *she* think he's having an affair?"

"She just does." Her voice sharp now. "*Do* something."

"I'll pop round tomorrow," said Frank.

He put the phone down, shaking his head, a sensation of a smile on his face. It broadened into a proper smile as he remembered the first time this conversation had occurred. He had been twelve. His mother, out of boredom more than anything else he now realised, had decided that his father was having an affair. She had paid Frank five pounds to trail him one evening. Frank had adored it. He had loitered happily in the darkness following his father from work, to home, to the pub, back home, out to the shop. His father had not been having an affair then, nor was he now. He was an upright, fiercely loyal and loving man, who adored Frank's mother, despite her somewhat eccentric views.

This incident would have come to nothing had it not been for Mrs Johnson. Mrs Johnson was one of his mother's cronies. They met in the tearooms on Friday mornings to talk. Frank had been fifteen that summer day when his mother had returned home full of her news.

"She's sure Brian is having an affair. Absolutely. No proof, of course. Get out!" she'd snapped as Frank had begun to rummage through the shopping bags. "Why don't you do something useful instead of hanging round under my feet all day." Her voice had trailed off, a gleam had entered her eye. And that was how Frank had found himself on his bicycle following Mr Johnson round the town.

Mrs Johnson's suspicions had been correct. She had paid Frank for his work, filed for divorce, and promised to recommend him to all her friends. Looking back now

Frank appreciated the irony of the past, but did not regret it. Blessed with Frank's strong sense of the value of truth and his obsession to know and understand people, the business had blossomed.

He sat down at the old desk, salvaged from a local estate agent who had gone bust. He ran his hands over the green leather. The reassurance of simple actions brought his mind into focus. He scribbled himself a quick note to drop in on his parents tomorrow, and snapped the computer on.

Though it would be possible to track Kevin down and simply ask him why he had hanged the dogs, Frank knew this would produce only a brick wall. He remembered the shifts of air around the tree, the sense of a person teetering on the edge. A slight breeze could dislodge that fragile safety. No. This must be trodden round lightly and probed only gently from some faraway point. If he were capable of hanging three dogs who could say what else he might do. Could too hard a push drive him to worse violence? Frank thought of Alison. But not just straightforward violence, twisted violence. Frank thought of himself, his racehorse, and finally of Annie.

The computer whirred, gave a gentle sigh and lit up. Frank waited for it patiently, turning the glass in his hand, feeling its contours beneath his fingertips. He launched himself onto the world wide web.

He read a report by some German analyst on the motivation behind animal killing. But despite its length and excessive use of long words all it actually said was that it was usually the result of some childhood trauma. This was one of Frank's least favourite expressions. He ground his teeth. The mood passed.

He read of cats being maimed and tortured and of dogs being mutilated. But this act of Kevin's had not been about the animals. This was not an action aimed at them, but rather at those that loved them. Devious and devastatingly spot-on. Maximum impact.

Sickened by the images before him, he turned off the computer and crossed the room to look at the photo once more. But his brain was clouding with dismembered bodies, and outrage was clouding his thoughts. Knowing this mood from old, Frank turned off the lights and made his way to bed.

INCHING HIS WAY past three rotting cars and through an excess of mud the next morning, Frank thought the description 'garage' a little generous. A few chickens scratched feebly at the gritty ground. An old Ford lay hunched in the middle of the yard. Its bonnet open, its engine spilling over the sides like guts. An old man appeared round the side of one of the dilapidated sheds that framed the yard.

"Can I help you?"

"Are you Stanley?" asked Frank.

"Depends who's asking." The man grinned at him, revealing yellow teeth.

Frank had dressed with care for this excursion, choosing a bland sweater and slacks and placing on his nose a pair of round tortoiseshell glasses. The overall effect made him look, as Annie had put it, like a drip. Good, he'd replied, before letting himself out of the house.

"I um," Frank twisted his hands nervously, forcing a slight blush across his cheeks. "Someone said you might be able to help me."

"Perhaps," said the old man, wiping his hands on an oil-stained rag. "If you tell me the problem."

"Well," Frank peered confidingly at the man. "I lent someone some money and, well..." he flustered.

The old man snorted.

"That was stupid then, weren't it? Who did you lend it to?"

"Um, Kevin, Kevin Todd?"

The old man laughed outright this time.

"That was really bloody stupid weren't it? You ain't gonna see hide nor hair of that again now are you?" He beamed kindly at Frank. "Coffee?"

Perched tentatively on a rickety kitchen chair, Frank let his eyes drift round the small room. Old faded photos of cows layered the walls and framed certificates appeared between them.

"Had to sell," said the old man. "Son wanted to work with computers. Idiot. Here." He plonked a mug down on the table. The coffee spilt. Frank was reminded sharply of Alison. Gradually he brought the conversation round to Kevin.

"Been round here a fair while. Gives me a hand now and then. Good worker, bit light-fingered though, if you know what I mean. Then calls me senile when I say things have gone walkies. But we can't all be perfect. Makes me laugh at least. Always got a nice pretty girl with him as well, if you know what I mean? Heh." The old man chuckled to himself. Frank cringed.

"Came from Nottingham. Think maybe a bit of trouble there. Women kicking up over nothing. Just like my Josie."

After a half-hour monologue on the subject of the old man's estranged wife, Frank stumbled gratefully into the sunlight and reached the safety of his car.

As FRANK MEANDERED along the lanes from his parents' house to Alison's, he thought about his mother. She had been her usual brilliantly irrational self, berating him for not working and then keeping him there for hours jabbering on about this and that and nothing. She was, he reflected, a superb liar. This led him to an old and familiar thought, but one that still intrigued him. If you were capable of lying, then were you by definition capable of greater crimes? His mother lied merely to make life more entertaining, but Frank would have wagered his right arm on her doing no more than that. But could you ever truly know what somebody was capable of? And indeed, could you ever truly know another person? The image of Kevin presented by the old man was a world apart from the one presented by Alison. By implication, Stanley at the garage had deemed him to be a lovable rogue. Not a high level criminal, just a slightly bent man. Where did you draw the line? How could you class someone as an innocent crook? Could you really know that was all they were capable of? Or was the first step the hardest? Steal a hammer, rob a man, kill a man?

The gravel scrunched under the tyres as he turned his car into Alison's driveway. He climbed out and looked down. By his feet lay a tennis ball. He picked it up and felt the teeth marks from where a proud dog had carried its trophy. An innocent crook. He felt the thud of anger as the front door opened, but it was washed aside by compassion as he looked down into Alison's eyes. Her eyes swept downwards to the ball and she flinched. A tiny gasp escaped. He raised his hand to give her the ball and she flinched again.

"Are you okay?" he asked.

She nodded mutely, holding her hand out for the ball. He handed it to her and she grabbed it, rolling it in her hands. He watched the desolation pour down her face as her fingers encountered the marks made by their teeth. Gently he drew her inside. Sat her down.

She watched him moving softly round the kitchen. He was much quieter, much stiller than Kevin. Even the kettle seemed to boil more gently under his touch. Kevin had stood there. She could see him so clearly that the walls seemed to fade by comparison. His body throbbing with colour, light and vitality, so that when he moved the room seemed to sway with him, follow him, drawn towards his power, his strength. But now the colours seemed muted, sad.

"Here you are," said Frank.

He hadn't used her mug. She wrapped her hands round its warmth.

"You've got a few days off work?" he asked.

Gentle questions soothing her, wrapping her in layers of facts.

"I went to see Stanley Jones, the man with the garage," said Frank. Having calmed her down, he could now question and probe.

Stanley, she remembered now. He had taken her there one Saturday to pick up some tools that Stanley had borrowed. She remembered the chickens and the sweet little kitchen and the pictures of the cows. They had drunk coffee. She had sat by him. His thigh pulsing on hers, so that the coffee seemed tasteless. The sense of touch so powerful that it rendered the others mere shadows. They hadn't picked up the tools and when she'd reminded him in the yard, he'd laughed and kissed her. His breath filling her, completing her. Tools forgotten, they had returned to the car and driven into the woods where it was quiet and only the birds sang sorrowfully, no, joyfully in the trees.

"Stanley insinuated that Kevin pinched his tools," said Frank idly, though his eyes were trained fiercely on her face.

"No," she said, looking up at him, a sleepy smile on her face. His hands twisting around her, snaking up her thighs. "He used to lend Stanley tools, help him out. Stanley's senile," she giggled.

Senile Stanley, he'd said one evening. Yet again convinced I'd pinched his tools. Honestly the man doesn't know what day of the week it is. They laughed, together. Together. The word stabbed now.

Frank watched her. Her face moved, recalling, recounting the days. He frowned. Exhaustedly sad, he yawned.

"How's Laura?" he asked.

Alison shrugged, jerked out of her own reminiscences.

"Same as usual. Moody."

Frank smiled reassuringly at her.

"You could get a puppy," he said. The words leaving his mouth without thought. She looked at him, her eyes wide. Then she smiled.

ONE STORY, HE THOUGHT LATER, safely ensconced in his office. One story, many different viewpoints. Stanley, Alison and Kevin. Like a kaleidoscope they fragmented around him. But was Kevin causing this fragmentation of the past, or was that simply an effect of the nature of human beings? Did we always distort events? Picking only the good, omitting the bad? Lying not only to one another but to ourselves? Subconsciously maybe, but with the conscious mind we all believed our version was true. So if we take all the fragments and place them together, will a real picture emerge? The picture behind the kaleidoscope. Or was that simply lost?

He had to know. Following a thought that had occurred the day before, he turned on the computer. He brought up the online archives for the *Nottingham Evening News*. Eager now, he typed in the words and waited. And then it appeared, dated twenty-eight years ago.

> City councillor James Young, of 12 Finchley Road, was shocked on Monday morning to discover the bodies of his three family dogs hanging from a tree in his garden. The Young family were too distressed to comment. Neighbour Mrs Jane White told the *News*, "This is quite appalling. This is a nice neighbourhood. Whoever did this is a pervert and must be caught and brought to justice." A police spokesman said detectives were looking into the incident.

Frank scrolled furiously through the following weeks' editions. But there was no further mention of the incident. Nothing. All he had was a name. James Young.

He rang the number provided by directory enquiries.

"Hello?" The voice wavered.

Frank spoke softly, voicing his question.

"They moved dear." The voice barely reached him. "Wait."

There was a long silence. Frank half considered hanging up. But there was the paddling sound of feet along the corridor.

"Here you are," said the lady. "Been there all those years."

And as she read him the address, Frank blessed the war generation, that had been taught to save everything.

James Young, 2 Seaview Road, Fratton, Cornwall.

Frank sat back. He heard his heart thump. It had happened before. It had to be Kevin. Frank longed to rush to Cornwall, but it was too late. Reluctantly he made his way to bed. He knew he would not be able to sleep.

HE MUST HAVE SLEPT, for there was sunlight dancing on the floorboards when he awoke and his dreams seemed to linger in the room. He could not grasp them, only a sense of greyness that hovered at the edge of his mind. He shook himself roughly.

In the kitchen Annie was staring sleepily out of the window. The kettle had boiled and the smell of coffee drove the last of the greyness out of Frank's mind.

"You'll make someone a lovely wife someday," he teased, as she poured him coffee.

"What have you found?" she asked, her eyes focusing in on him.

"What do you mean?"

"Don't know," she yawned. "You've got that suppressed anticipation. Glee almost."

Frank looked proudly at his daughter.

"Go back to bed. You're too perceptive. I'll tell you later, if all goes well."

HE THOUGHT ABOUT his daughter and his wife as he headed his car south. Kate had left abruptly two months ago and headed off to some commune in the French Alps. He had been devastated. Kate had called it a *realisation*, he called it desertion, but Annie, she had called it an episode. He remembered his embarrassment at his own daughter finding him crying. She hasn't left you, Annie had said, she's left the world. And even now he could see how she shaped the world with her hands, and made it bearable. They had hugged, united in a way they had never been. Quiet, but strangely articulate with it, she daily seemed to reveal herself to him. It was largely her perception that astonished him, unusual in one so young, though she was now seventeen. Growing up, he thought sadly, remembering her as a small child, running, her tiny face filled with joy and intense concentration.

His mind slipped sideways to Laura and Alison. Hard to know what their relationship had been like before. Alison seemed so vague when questioned about her daughter: as if her mind were overcome with Kevin. A pity the events had not brought them closer together. He would, he reflected, be interested to know Laura's true thoughts on Kevin, rather than the barbed remarks, aimed at her mother, that she had made about him. With each fragment a picture might emerge. Or so he hoped.

Anticipation made him drive faster as he drew closer to Cornwall. Familiar now, the scent of the chase, yet it never failed to excite him in some childish way. No different really from hide and seek. Fratton lay sleepily in the autumnal sunlight. The smell of the sea hit him and he wound his windows right down, drawing in great gulps of the salty air. He passed down the high street. Two women with buggies stood chatting on the pavement, a middle-aged couple strolled quietly. Frank consulted his map and soon found himself in a wide street overlooking the sea. Modern houses sat peacefully in large gardens. He stopped outside number two and cut the engine. Climbing out he stretched, feeling his back uncurl. The silence was soporific.

He followed the path to the door and rang the bell. A *mêlée* of barking ensued, followed by a gruff male voice berating the dogs. The door opened a crack.

"Good morning Mr Young," said Frank.

"What are you selling?" asked the man. A dog whined.

"Nothing," said Frank. The door opened a further inch. "I'd like to talk to you about your dogs," said Frank.

"Are you from the Council?"

"No."

"What have they done then?"

"No," said Frank, "not these dogs. The other dogs. In Nottingham."

There was a silence. Frank heard a thump as one of the dogs sat down. Then only silence again. The door opened. An old man stood in the doorway. He had a slight hunch, as if the years bore down on him, and his hands shook slightly. His hair was silver and brushed neatly back, cruelly emphasising the gauntness of his face. The dogs weaved around his legs.

"You best come in then," said Mr Young.

The kitchen was bright and orderly. The surfaces gleamed and the dogs circled round Frank fighting for his admiration. He stroked them absentmindedly.

"She's just had pups," said Mr Young, pointing at the chocolate labrador. Frank patted her, she looked up at him, trusting. Her eyes reminded Frank of Alison, loyal, loving.

"Your other dogs," said Frank, drawing the man back into the past.

James Young looked at Frank, his eyes suddenly narrow.

"How did you find out?" he asked.

"The internet," replied Frank, almost ashamed.

James Young nodded. He remained silent, waiting for Frank to take the lead.

"Do you know who did it?" asked Frank. His breath felt laboured.

James Young nodded. Frank watched his fingers tighten around the labrador beside him. "Kevin Todd," he said.

Frank breathed, his lungs releasing the air in one vast motion.

"How do you know?" asked Frank.

James Young looked at him.

"Why are you here?" he asked. His voice was sharp, the panic of an old man alone in his house with a stranger. They were still standing either side of the kitchen table and the dogs gathered round James's legs like troops supporting their general.

"He did it again," said Frank. The three patches of bare earth.

James nodded. There was no surprise in his eyes. "I wondered," he said. "I wondered." He struggled with the words. "I wondered when it would happen again."

When, Frank noted, not if.

"Why did you think it would happen again?" asked Frank.

"It was such a precise action. So much impact. So unlike the person you thought he was. Controlled even."

"Why did he do it?" asked Frank, gently nudging Mr Young back on track.

"Do what?" asked James. "Biscuit?" he offered, forgetting his previous panic. Frank took one and ate it, gathering his thoughts.

"What was he like?" asked Frank.

"Polite, well-spoken, kind, concerned, everything you want your daughter's boyfriend to be."

"He was your daughter's boyfriend?"

"Yes," said James. "I told you that." He looked crossly at Frank.

"How old was she?"

"My wife is dead," said James. His eyes were moist.

"I'm sorry," said Frank. "How old was your daughter when she went out with Kevin Todd?"

"Sixteen. He took her out. To the cinema, to the shops. For lunch. He was older, had a car. A Ford. I never liked Fords myself, but there's no accounting for taste." James chewed his biscuit thoughtfully. "We had an MG," he said finally.

"That's nice," said Frank. "Does your daughter live with you?"

"Fenella. Her name is Fenella."

"Fenella," repeated Frank. "Does she live..."

"I heard you the first time," said James sharply. "No she doesn't. She lives in..." His voice trailed off. Frank saw the confusion cloud his eyes.

"How did you know it was Kevin who killed your dogs?" asked Frank again.

James was frowning now, the past growing hazy around him.

"Fenella said." His voice had changed now, confused. "Ask her. I don't know. I can't remember."

"It's okay," said Frank. He patted James's hand. His eyes focused again.

"Is there anything else you can tell me?" asked Frank.

James frowned. The past swooped away from him. Something hovered. Frank saw it cross the surface of James's eye.

"What?" asked Frank pouncing.

"A photo," said James, but the thought fell through his fingers into the chasm of an old man's memory.

"Thank you," said Frank, as coherence struggled against knowledge.

"Would you like a puppy?" said James Young.

TO JAMES YOUNG, Kevin was polite, well mannered, thought Frank as he drove home. To Stanley, he was a lovable rogue. To Alison he was funny, charming, adorable. So far, he had been three different men. Cling to the facts. His name was Kevin Todd. He had hanged three dogs in Nottingham twenty-eight years ago and three in the Midlands on Sunday. They were facts. But what of the time in between? What of those years? Were there other stories, other faces? But still the question: why? Alison did not know, Mr Young did not know, but Fenella might, thought Frank.

ALISON MET HIM AT THE DOOR. In her arms lay a puppy. It squirmed, exquisitely joyful. He smiled at her. She smiled back, but the smile fell as she remembered another puppy, another man. He'd chosen it, picked it out, brought it home. She remembered him in the doorway, delighted with his gift. She hadn't wanted another puppy. But she'd loved it. Alison's face drained, she turned from the doorway, padded across the hallway into the kitchen. She rocked the puppy like a baby, crooning softly to it. Maternal love flooding her face. She must be a very loving mother, thought Frank. The compassion filled her eyes as teardrops.

The kitchen door swung open. Laura stood there. Despite the relative warmth of the day she was encased in jumpers, her hands screwed up in the sleeves. For a brief moment she looked at Frank, her face young, open, defenceless, then it shut down. Her eyes flicked to her mother and then to the puppy. She held out her hands. Reluctantly Alison relinquished the animal.

Frank was struck by the resemblance between mother and daughter. The way her arms curled around the small bundle. How her fingers laced in its fur. Her knuckles gleamed dully white through her skin. She sank to the floor, engrossed. He watched her hands move in small circles across its belly, the motion appearing to soothe her.

She grew still. The puppy lay sleepily on its back, its legs sprawled, its gesture as open as the mother and daughter were closed.

Alison looked away from her daughter and up at Frank, as if noticing his presence for the first time.

"Shall we have a drink?" she said. Without waiting for an answer, she poured three glasses of whiskey. They watched him, their eyes wary now. They had seen the gleam of excitement in his face and wondered what it might mean. Frank turned his glass in his hand. The whiskey bit at his throat.

"Well?" said Alison. The word hung between them. Time on a thread. She had reached the line. A pulse through her body pushed the last fear of knowledge aside. "Why?"

"I don't know," he replied.

"Well what then?" asked Alison, her eyes fluttering in confusion and disappointment.

"It happened before," said Frank. His eyes twitched between them. He saw the flutter in Alison's eyes, but Laura's were turned away, transfixed on the puppy, only her hand stilled.

"Yes?" said Alison. She leaned towards him. Her breath smelt sour.

"Twenty-eight years ago," said Frank softly.

"Twenty-eight years ago?" she echoed, drawing away from him. He took a sip of his whiskey and waited. Then she spilled over.

"Why? Why so long ago? What about the years in between?" He felt her body tense and scrabbling. Broken anticipation.

"I don't know," he said gently. He placed his hands on her shoulders, feeling her sag beneath him.

"Why?" She turned on him, accusing, hating, as if she could transfer her pain by looks alone. He wished he could take it, but he could not.

"Because Mr Young, whose dogs they were, doesn't know."

"Oh." Her mouth dropped, the flashing anger passing, leaving her cold and alone. And in her head he walked. His back towards her. But when he turned she could not see his face.

"Please." Her eyes looked up at him. Beseeching.

"I will try to find out," he said. No need to tell her of his throbbing desire to know. No need to fan her flames with his own. Quiet. Soft. Be gentle with her, balancing on the edge.

She was crying now, gentle sobs, the tears streaming down her cheeks.

"I can't see his face," she said. "I'm losing him, he's breaking up, dispersing. I have to know him."

"So do I," muttered Frank, but too quietly for her to hear.

Laura sat quite still. Her hair covered her face and Frank could not see her eyes.

The puppy suddenly bounded up, leaping across the room, chasing the sunlight that danced across the floor. For a moment all three watched the puppy, losing themselves in its own joy, its own delight, that this was life, here and now. Its unconsciousness in its own body. It pounced and looked up. The innocence hurt. They looked away.

"I want," said Alison, her voice steady now, a trace of steel, "I want to know everything."

4

"DAD!" said Annie crossly.

"What?" He turned towards her, his body still slumped back in his chair.

"I've been talking to you for hours and you haven't taken a word in."

"Hours?" he said, smiling.

"You know what I mean." She resisted the temptation to stamp her foot. Her mother's face, screwed up in frustration, appeared unbidden in her mind. Annie smiled at her father.

"Sorry," he said. "What were you trying to tell me?"

"Nick rang about Benny. He's running on Saturday. You need to ring Andrew and let him know. Please can I come?"

Frank's eyes flitted to the photograph of his racehorse, Benny. Given to him to pay off a bad debt by an aging lady, Benny was the one thing that could distract him from a case. He pushed his hair back off his face and looked at his daughter. She bounced on the balls of her feet in anticipation and Frank could see a flash of her mother's annoyance in her eyes.

"Of course," he smiled.

"ANDREW."

"Frank, how are you?"

"Good. Benny's running on Saturday."

"Great. Must go. Meeting."

Slowly Frank replaced the handset. He picked up the photograph on his desk and frowned. He needed to speak to Alison again. To probe and delve to get more of a sense of the man and his past. Now that the initial shock had passed and been replaced by something harder, he felt that the balance had shifted. Up until then she had been defensive about Kevin as if still protecting his memory—and even him. But now she was on the attack, and maybe he could learn more.

"Bye Dad," shouted Annie from the hallway. The front door slammed shut, sending a slight breeze through the house. He slipped the photo into a drawer as if he did not trust the picture itself and left the house.

AS HE DROVE, he thought of what Alison had told him and what he needed to ask. He knew that Kevin had come from Nottingham, that his parents were dead, and he knew about the dogs. But, thought Frank, who can say that those meagre facts were the truth. And how can you investigate a life built on lies—would it simply not just collapse when touched? Perhaps.

He parked his car and climbed out. As he slammed the car door, the front door opened.

"Morning," said Frank.

Alison simply nodded and turned away, indicating that he should follow. He watched her back as he followed her to the kitchen. Noticed something harder than yesterday, a trace of uprightness. Focused. The vertebrae at the base of her neck stood out, the bones pressing harshly against the flesh.

"Coffee?" she asked, turning towards him. He nodded, his eyes upon her face. He noted the make-up, the carefully arranged hair, the control. Only her eyes she could not control and he watched them scurry, caged animals, held in by the tightness of her face.

"I've been trying to think," she said without preamble.

"Good," he nodded.

"I've tried to remember everything, no matter how small, or how insignificant it appears."

He nodded his head again encouragingly and gestured for her to continue. She stood up and left the room. She reappeared with a notepad and sat down. He waited patiently while she lit a cigarette. But she did not speak.

"What did you find?" he asked finally.

"Nothing really," she said. But she would not hold his gaze.

"What?" he asked, leaning forwards.

"I said nothing really," she said.

Frank leant back, cursing himself for his pushiness.

"Please," he said. "I'd like to know, however small."

"Well," she said. He watched her mouth tighten. "There are two odd things that I remember. But they're probably nothing." Hanging onto hope.

Frank gestured for her to continue.

"We hadn't been together very long and we'd gone to a local pub. My friend was singing there. Kevin wandered off. Then came back, said we were going, dragged me out. A girl followed us. Crying." Alison stopped. There was something blank in her expression. The dark street. His fingers curled round her arm, clutching to the bone, and the girl's heels clicking on the pavement behind them.

"Did you ask what it was about?"

"Yes," she said, frowning.

"And?"

"Nothing. He said it was nothing."

"Did you believe him?"

"I don't know. I can't remember." She shook her head, wiping the unease.

Frank sighed.

"The other incident?"

She lit another cigarette.

"I had been sent out of the office to go and see an old housebound lady. I was driving back on some country lane and I saw his car. I stopped. Thought I would surprise him." Something, maybe shame, crossed her face. Frank tensed. "He was on his mobile. Shouting. Really shouting. I waited. He must have hung up on whoever it was. I called him. He spun round."

"Was he pleased to see you?" asked Frank.

"No," she said. "He looked." She grappled for the right word. "Alarmed. I think." She stopped and peered out of the window. "I'm sure it's nothing. I'm probably just over-reacting, reading too much into things. He always said I did that. Mountain out of a molehill." She smiled a lazy smile. His voice in her head warmed her, caressed her.

"Tell me about the first time you met," said Frank.

THE NARROW TOWN HOUSE. Winter. Unlocking the door. Tired. The sound of water. The squelching underfoot. She had run out, down the street to Marsha. Banging on the door. Bursting in. And there he had been. Lounging against the stove. His hands curled round a mug. The gently rising steam framing his face. A cowboy's hat pulled down low over his eyes. The width of his shoulders filling his shirt. His neck rising gracefully out of the collar, meeting the striking blond hair that brushed his shoulders. His laugh from a moment before, lingering in the air. My pipes have burst, she had said. Her eyes upon him. Kevin will fix them. Marsha's voice hovering round her ears. Distant. His hand slipping into hers as they left the house as if that was where it should be, where it belonged. She'd watched him work. The disaster suddenly a riotous joke. Laura coming home. The house suddenly full. Alive as it had never been. Fish and chips. The taste so strong and vital. The colours throbbing. The laughter. And later. Entwined. Gasping breaths. And something thudding through her body. Speechlessly drifting. Enfolded by colours. Good, he'd said. Half statement, half question. Nodding mutely. Her body. Flung as a rag doll. Sprawled. His eyes skimming her. Triumphant. Entangled they had slept.

"DID YOU NOT find it strange that he moved straight in?" asked Frank.

"No," said Alison.

"What about his own house?"

"He didn't have a house."

"Really? A grown man, with no house?"

She flushed.

"He was living in a caravan. He'd sold his house and hadn't bought another one yet."

"I see," said Frank, twisting his pen round his fingers.

"It's true," said Alison, her voice grabbing at the words.

"Yes," said Frank, brushing her assertions aside. "And this house? Who owns it?"

"I do."

"But what about his money? Laura implied that you supported him. Did you?"

She looked away down the garden.

"It's my money," she said. "I can spend it how I want."

"Of course you can," said Frank. He smiled, softening his face.

She slumped.

"And how long have you been here?" asked Frank.

"Eighteen months roughly."

"So you moved here not long after you met?"

"Yes."

"And you'd planned to move here before you'd met him?"

"No."

"Oh." Frank waited for her to fill the silence.

"I was going to move to a tiny cottage in a village. But it would have been too small. So we came here." Frank looked at her. "But I love it here," she said.

"Not many close neighbours," commented Frank idly. Alison looked at him. But his eyes rested lazily on his pen.

"I know. Aren't we lucky," she said staunchly.

"Do you like people?" asked Frank. His eyes flicked over her. He noticed her start.

"Yes," she said. The word came out a little too loud, making her jump.

"Your neighbours?" he said gently, quietly.

"They keep themselves to themselves really," she said. The words slipped away. He nodded.

"Did you ever meet any of his family?"

"I told you his parents died."

"Siblings. Cousins."

"He was an only child." He watched a glimmer of doubt sidle across her face. "Not a close family."

"Did that strike you as odd?"

"No. Lots of families aren't close."

"But then people usually have a close-knit group of friends. A replacement family. Did he have that?"

"He had me." Her eyes were moist now.

"But before you?"

"I don't know!" she snapped. He leant back in his chair.

"He came from Nottingham?"

"Yes," she said. Her voice small now.

"Okay," said Frank.

Alison slumped passively in her chair. Frank watched her.

"You were just divorced when you met Kevin?"

She nodded. He saw a flutter in the corner of her eye. He pressed forwards. "How did you feel after your divorce? Sad, low self-confidence, lonely?" She nodded silently. "And he made you feel special, loved, beautiful?" She was crying now. He watched the tears spill over her eyelids and course down her face. "You would have done anything for him?" She nodded again. "Done anything not to lose him?"

She turned to him. Her cheeks wet with tears. Her eyes red.

"I loved him."

"I know," said Frank, with a sigh. "I know."

They sat in silence. Outside the wind had picked up. The noise wrapped itself around the cottage as if sealing it from the outside world. Frank waited. Her words spun softly in his head. Marsha.

"Tell me about Marsha," he said.

"Marsha?" She looked at him, a slight flush upon her cheeks. "Why?"

"She knew him before you."

"She didn't know him." Shouting in her mind, she pushed the sounds away. "Not like I did."

"No," agreed Frank, "but she must have known him a little."

"Yes," she concurred.

"Well?" said Frank.

"Marsha was my friend. She lived down the road. I'd known her before my divorce."

"Is she no longer your friend?" Frank's voice was light but his eyes rested sharply upon her.

Alison looked up, her eyes tight.

"What do you mean?"

"Have you seen much of her recently?"

"I've been busy."

"Did Kevin like her?"

Alison smiled, his voice sharp in her mind. *Interfering old cow*, he'd said.

"Not really." She grinned. Memories warmed her.

Frank wanted to shake her. Blind. How could she not see what was written in front of her? How could she not know what was true?

"Where does Marsha live?" he asked.

FRANK LOOKED AT THE NARROW HOUSE where Alison had lived. He walked further down the street. He reached number twelve. It was a large house, an old house. Big grubby windows filled the front, framing the carved oak door. Frank raised the knocker. Green with age. The door opened. A lady stood there. Middle aged, wild grey hair swept back into a child's hair band before tumbling round her shoulders. She wore a man's shirt, covered with paint, and no trousers. The eyes that looked up at him were green and large. Amused.

"Marsha Lane?" said Frank.

"Indeed," said the lady. Her voice was well spoken, summoning up visions of tweeds and twin sets. Directly at odds with her garb, Frank smiled.

"My name is Frank Hargreaves, I'm a private detective. Would it be possible to talk to you?"

The kitchen was generously proportioned. Splashed with colour and transfused with light. She watched him openly but without speaking, while she tipped wine carelessly into a glass. He sat quietly in a chair gazing in admiration at the paintings that covered the walls.

"Yours?" he said indicating to a vast canvas out of which rose a purple tree with green birds.

"Yes."

She sat opposite him.

"Why are you here?" she asked.

He smiled in the face of such openness.

"I wanted to talk to you about Kevin Todd."

Her eyes flashed momentarily, though with anger or pain he could not tell.

"Kevin," she said, her voice blank. "Why?"

"I'm investigating him."

"For Ali I presume." Marsha sighed. "I told her. I told her." She looked at him and smiled sadly. "But there is no satisfaction in being right. What's he done?"

"It's not very nice," said Frank softly.

"Obviously. Else you would not be here. Tell me."

He told her. Watched her face spill from one emotion to the next. Anger, sorrow, grief, compassion, rage.

"Poor Ali," she said finally.

"Can you tell me about him?" asked Frank.

Marsha got up and crossed the room, she rummaged in a drawer and pulled out a pack of cigarettes.

"I'm meant to be giving up," she said, flicking the lighter. She inhaled deeply. "Kevin. Where do I start?"

"Your instincts?" suggested Frank.

"I've known Kevin a while. He is amusing I'll grant him that. But profoundly untrustworthy." She frowned.

"In what way?"

"Lying, stealing. Never on a large scale, just small things, but somehow that seems worse. Like Chinese water torture, a slow drip drip of lies, not even lies, more half-truths. The deadliest form of lying. He's a drifter I think. He appeared round here years ago and became the name on everyone's lips. Kevin. He does odd jobs, this and that, mainly for single women. Not a man's man if you get my drift."

"Were you sleeping with him?" asked Frank.

"I don't think that that is the sort of question you should ask a lady."

Frank looked at Marsha. The green eyes glared back at him, but her mouth curled in undisguised humour. "Yes," she said, "I was. But," she held up her hand, "you must understand the difference. I regarded him as fun. I was not sucked into his little world. He hated it. I was only an in-between thing. A stepping-stone between one conquest and the next. Then Alison walked through my door." Marsha shook her head. "I saw them look at each other. Bam. Guilt's a bugger. If only."

"It's not your fault," said Frank.

"I know," said Marsha, lighting a new cigarette off the butt of the old one. "But there's something about Alison, she's so sweet, unworldly, an innocent. You want to protect her. I know I must sound so derogatory, but she looked so young standing in my doorway, wide open eyes, and he loomed over her, predatory. How could she defend herself?"

"Did you try to tell her?"

Marsha nodded and took a long drag on her cigarette. He watched her turn it in her hands.

"I was too late," she said simply. "He had already got her."

She stood up and crossed the floor. Frank watched her bare feet on the flagstones.

The dust creeping round her toes. The muscles tightening in her calves as she strained on tiptoes to reach the drinks cupboard. A strong lady, he thought, mentally and physically. Wise too. She mixed him a gin and tonic. The taste filled him, leaving him empty.

"What are you trying to find?" she asked. Her fingers made patterns on the table top.

"She wants to know him, all of him, no more lies."

"So do you," said Marsha, her green eyes holding his. He nodded. "And you will," said Marsha, "you will."

She showed him her paintings. The swirling, flashing colours revived him. Filling him with their light and their passion.

"It's my daughter's birthday soon," he said. "Maybe I could bring her to choose one?"

"You're a good man," said Marsha. They stopped in front of a tiny picture. A single petal in a pool of water. "There are not many good people around."

"Did you know Alison's husband, Jason?" asked Frank.

Marsha grunted.

"You didn't get on I take it?"

"Boring, was not the word. And worst of luck, not only was he boring and hence safe, but he proved not to be safe either and ran off with some little bimbo."

"I'm sorry," said Frank.

"What for? The deficiencies of your gender? I can hardly blame you for that, now can I. Now this your daughter might like." They stopped again in front of a seascape. The waves threatened to spill out of the canvas.

"I get seasick," said Frank, moving on. "Do you know if Kevin was faithful to Alison?"

"I very much doubt it," snapped Marsha.

"Did you continue sleeping with him?" asked Frank.

Marsha looked at him.

"You're too bloody perceptive," she said.

They returned to the kitchen. She looked older suddenly, the light dimmed somewhat in her eyes. She mixed more drinks.

"There is something drug-like about him. You crave him. I can't really explain. You just feel as if you have to have him. I am not excusing myself, I'm trying to show you what effect he had on people."

"When did you last see him?"

"Six months ago," she said. "I'm out of rehab now." Her mouth smiled at her joke, but her eyes remained down turned. "At least when you come off heroin they give you methadone. There is no replacement drug for this."

"How did you manage?"

"I painted and painted and painted. I'm free now." She laughed flatly.

"Kevin told Alison that he had a house and had sold it to live in a caravan. Is that true?"

Marsha laughed.

"No. The caravan part maybe. I never asked. Never wanted to know. But he had no money. He lived off women."

"Did he live off you?"

She shook her head.

"I'm not like the women he lived off."

"In what sense?"

"He liked submissive, insecure people whom he could mould."

"Why did he like you, then?" asked Frank.

"I don't really know," she replied. "I think," she said slowly, "I represented some form of stability for him. An escape from his endless circle of admiration. An escape from his own form of escapism."

"Interesting," said Frank. "What about the rumours you mentioned?"

"They were mostly about women. Women who'd lost money, or pride. But it is hard to separate vengeance from truth. I don't put any faith in rumours."

"Do you know where he came from?" asked Frank.

Marsha leant against the window. The dusky evening light slipped past her frame, so that she was but a silhouette against the dimness.

"Nottingham, I think," she said.

"I'VE COOKED SUPPER, DAD," said Annie, as he stepped in from the outside.

"Thank you darling."

"Do you want a drink? I bought some wine to go with supper." She hovered anxiously, poised between childhood and adulthood.

Frank smiled at her.

Annie flushed.

"You know they never ask for I.D."

Frank smiled again. He knew he should not have another drink. The gin-and-tonics had slipped into his bloodstream too easily. But the earlier rage fuelled by Alison had crept back, and the desire to blot out the day was too pressing.

Annie carefully poured two glasses of wine. He watched her, thinking of Marsha.

"Would you like a painting for your birthday?" he asked.

"Depends," said Annie, frowning in concentration at her cooking.

"On what?"

"Whether I like it."

"I think you'd like this lady's work," he replied.

They ate in silence. Frank focused on his food, trying to detach his mind from Kevin. But the images swam up, uncontrollably. He felt overwhelmed. Other people's lives upon his shoulders, the years like building blocks.

He carried on drinking after supper and long into the night. Alone in his office he watched the light slip away. And gradually the tension that he had absorbed from Alison and Marsha began to drift away.

It was only when he stood up that he realised quite how drunk he was.

ALISON STOOD SILENTLY in the bedroom doorway and watched her sleeping daughter. She lay tightly curled around the puppy, which whimpered in its sleep but did not stir. Reluctantly she made her way to bed. But the memories that Frank had brought up would not settle. That pulse in her hand when first he had touched her coursed through her body, making her gasp. And Marsha. Marsha standing on the doorstep. The slam of the door. No. Kevin. She remembered waking the morning after and that flooding joy that had filled her. He'd opened one eye and smiled. And that smile alone had filled her. So light that she floated. So joyous that even the tiniest thing seemed beautiful. She had sung in the supermarket. I'll see you later, he'd said, wrapping himself around her in the doorway, until she was gasping for breath and giggling. And even Laura had smiled. That first weekend.

How did he do it? she thought suddenly, the cold touch of analysis piercing the gold of her memories, how did he make her feel like that? Bewitched. She shuddered against that word, forcing it away, letting herself drift back to the past. The minutes so laden with excitement and glee that they slipped, tumbling furiously, and time had never dragged. She no longer found herself staring at the clock watching the hands move just to prove that she was alive, that life really did continue. But the dogs. She pitched downwards out of her golden cloud. And found herself in the double bed, alone and in darkness.

FRANK WOKE WITH A HANGOVER. A tension round his forehead and a fuzziness on the edge of his vision. He cursed, groaning. Slowly he made his way downstairs.

"Morning," said Annie brightly.

He waved a hand and slumped down on a kitchen chair. She giggled at him.

Coffee and aspirin revived him. The iron band around his head eased and he felt his vision open outwards.

"How's it going?" asked Annie. "The case," she said, when he looked perplexed.

"Hard," he said, raking his fingers through his hair. "Like trying to find a tree in a forest."

"Shouldn't that be easy?" she asked, her head on one side.

"No. Not if you need to find a specific tree, without knowing which one you are looking for."

"Oh." She looked at her watch. "I better go."

FRANK TOOK HIS CUP OF COFFEE into his office and sat down. The morning sunlight splashed on his desk. He blinked. Like a mole, he thought. Blind. That word again. Applicable. Perhaps.

"Concentrate, Frank," he berated himself. He switched on the computer.

A while later he sat abruptly upright. Transfixed, he read the words before him again. Then wondered at his own surprise. Why did I think that he would have told the truth? Because, the answer pinged back from another section of his mind, we do. Instinctively. We always believe that other people are truthful, even despite evidence to the contrary. He craned forwards as if the words might disappear if not watched.

Kevin Todd, it said. Born to Jeremy Kevin Todd and Effie Katie Todd. There was a date of death recorded for Jeremy and indeed he had died when Kevin was young, but there was no date recorded for Effie. His mother was still alive.

THE NURSING HOME was in what would once have been a beautiful estate house, on the Welsh borders. But age had warped the building, leaving it tatty around the edges. Frank noted the dripping gutters, wonky tiles and unkempt grounds. Inside, though, the house had retained its former glory. He entered a vast hall. The floor covered in old tiles, the walls encased in oak panelling. The whole place warm and welcoming. In the distance the murmur of a television crept into the hallway. A stout lady in a blue uniform scuttled through the back end of the hall and someone was shouting.

"Agnes! Agnes! No!"

There was a crash of what sounded like china. This was shortly followed by uncontrollable cackles of laughter. Frank grinned. The house smelt clean, the flowers were fresh. As the commotion in the distance continued, Frank wandered to the unattended entrance desk and idly flicked through their brochure. This was no cheap nursing home. Who was paying for Effie? Certainly not Kevin. Unless he had some Robin Hood complex and lived off wealthy women to support his own mother. Frank smiled at the thought. Then he grimaced, cursing his imagination for betraying him, dragging him into fantasy. A door at the end of the hallway opened and a middle-aged lady appeared. Spotting him, she made her way slowly down the hall. Her heels clicked softly.

"Good afternoon," she said. "How may I help you?"

"Frank Hargreaves," he said, extending his hand. He smiled. "I phoned?"

"You did?" she flustered.

"About Effie. Effie Todd. The lady on the phone said it would be fine."

"It's not really visiting time," said the lady.

"I'm an old friend of the family," he said, hardening his voice. "I've made a long detour on the way to see my elderly mother. I was told there would be no problem." He stopped. Waited while she took in his well-cut suit, his tailored shirt. The briefcase. Elderly mother. He slipped his cuff back. A flash of a gold watch.

"Of course," said the lady, smiling graciously. "Do follow me."

She led him along the ground floor.

"These are our most popular rooms," she said as they passed open doorways.

"Very nice," said Frank.

The lady stopped by a closed door and knocked.

"Effie," she called softly. "Effie. There's a gentleman here to see you." She paused, then in an undertone. "You know she's a little senile, don't you."

"Of course," he smiled.

Effie Todd was sitting in a chair by the window. The ground outside slipped away down to a lake. He heard the lady's shoes click back down the corridor. He pulled up a chair and sat down beside her. She did not look round. Her gaze remained firmly trained out of the window. Frank looked round the room. The walls were uniform white and sparsely covered. An old photo of a man sat on the bedside table. Presumably Jeremy Todd. A painting of a tree. Uninspiring. And an old school photograph. Nottingham Grammar. 1973. Kevin.

"Lovely view isn't it?" said Frank, peering at the long grass.

"Um," she replied. Her hands twisted slowly in her lap.

"Have you been here long?" he asked. She turned her head slowly to look at him and then looked away without speaking.

"You lived in Nottingham before, didn't you Effie?"

"Nottingham," she repeated. He looked at her and saw she was crying.

"Effie," he said gently, placing his hand over her gnarled fingers.

"Such sweet children," she said.

"Who?" he asked.

"A thrush," said Effie, nodding her head towards the window. Frank looked. The bird sat on a branch of a nearby tree.

"I'm a friend of your son's, Effie." Her fingers quivered beneath his hand. A trapped bird. "Your son, Kevin."

"I have no son." And he no mother.

"What about Kevin?" said Frank.

"Kevin?"

"Your son."

"Such a sweet child."

"Who? Kevin?"

"Stop it!"

"Stop what, Effie?"

"Where's Kathy?"

"Who's Kathy?"

She turned her head again. The eyes now sharp.

"Who are you?"

"I'm Frank, a friend of your son's."

"Go away!" She screamed. Frank drew back startled. A frenzy of heels in the corridor. The door swung open.

"Effie, Effie. Sssh." A young nurse patted Effie's shoulder. Effie rocked backwards and forwards. The nurse glared at Frank.

"What did I do?" moaned Effie. "What did I do?"

"Come on," said the nurse brightly. "Time for a little lie-down I think." She got Effie to her feet. "I think you should leave," she said coldly to Frank.

"Goodbye," said Frank, from the doorway.

He retraced his steps down the corridor. The lady at the desk smiled at him.

"Everything okay Mr Hargreaves?"

Frank paused.

"She became rather anxious," he said sorrowfully.

"I am sorry. She does quite frequently I'm afraid. Nothing to do with you," she beamed kindly.

"She kept calling for Kathy."

"Yes. Her daughter. You know." The lady frowned at him, doubtful suddenly.

"Of course." Frank laughed. "I always called her Kay. Didn't connect. Silly."

"Easy mistake," said the lady. The frown left her forehead. Frank breathed.

"There was a son," he said slowly, questioningly.

The lady frowned. Puzzled.

"I didn't know she had a son," she said.

Frank sighed.

"Sadly age comes to us all."

WHAT A STUPID COMMENT, thought Frank, as he slid back into his car. He slipped it into gear and drove thankfully away. What had Kevin done that had caused his mother to wipe him from her mind? Maybe nothing. Maybe simply age had caused that tilt of reality. But that flutter in her fingers at the mention of his name. That had been real. As if the body still remembered what the mind did not. Perhaps he was reading too much into it. But something inside him had contracted. Her reaction had been too violent for there to be no cause. Something had happened. Something that had left a shell of a woman, screaming out at the mention of her son's name.

"You're lying," said Alison. Her eyes stared at him. He saw the anger, doubt, confusion, rotating in spirals around her. "No," she said. His voice in her head: *My parents died when I was eighteen. Left me all alone.* Her arms around him. Telling him he was safe, that she would look after him. Secure. That was what he had said. *You make me feel secure. You've given me a family.* His head on one side. That happy sad smile. Those eyes blanking out the world, so that they alone existed. Complete.

"Alison," said Frank, softly. She looked up. "I'm not lying. Why would I lie?"

"Why would *he* lie?" She threw it back at him. He wanted to shake her.

"To manipulate you."

"No!"

"Alison listen to me." His voice was hard now. "He lied to you. He cheated on you. He hanged your dogs. And that is only what I know."

"Cheated on me?" Her eyes wide rested on him. An innocent, Marsha had called her. How true. "What do you mean?" Her voice wandered, a lost child.

"He had affairs."

"No. He wouldn't. Not Kevin. He loved me."

"Alison." Frank felt his jaw tighten with frustration.

"Get out!" She stood up. Her finger trembled in the direction of the door.

"Alison," groaned Frank.

"Get out!" she screamed.

In the doorway he turned.

"Sooner or later," he said, "you will have to face the truth."

5

FRANK SHOOK HANDS with Hugo Macey, the trainer.

"Morning Frank."

Hugo looked liked a bear. Frank had been repelled by him on their first meeting, but over time had come to appreciate the man underneath.

"Nice day," said Hugo, placing one huge hand on Frank's shoulder and propelling him gently but firmly towards the owners' and trainers' tent.

They were at the races.

Frank and Annie set out. The tent was on the other side of the course. Despite the coolness of the day the sun was blazing. Spreading light across the turf. Frank breathed deeply. He felt the exasperation of the last few days finally start to seep into the ground.

"There's Andrew, Dad." Annie tugged at his sleeve, forcing him to hurry.

"Hello half-owner," said Andrew. Frank gave an attempt at a smile, though for him the joke was wearing very thin. Frank had been to forced to sell half his horse to Andrew to cover the costs. Benny had been placed in the money every time out since.

"Hi Andrew." Annie leant up and kissed him briefly on the cheek.

A sense of something half-shadowed crossed Frank's mind. But even as he turned searching for it, Andrew had thrust a drink into his hand and begun to regale him with some story about a mutual acquaintance. Frank turned the glass in his hand. His face framed in a posture of attentiveness.

"What's up?" said Andrew.

Frank looked at him, realising he must have missed the punch line of the story.

"Nothing," he said.

Andrew raised his eyebrows quizzically.

"Well stop staring into the distance and enjoy yourself then."

Frank forced a smile.

"Ignore him," said Annie giggling. "He's been like this all week. He got dumped."

"Dumped?" said Andrew.

"By a client," laughed Annie.

"I should think that would be a cause to celebrate," said Andrew, "having met some of his clients."

They laughed together, turning away into the crowd. Frank felt very cold. He walked away from the tent and leant on the railings. The runners for the first race cantered down to the start. Frank watched the horses' muscles as they moved. Piston-like their hooves thudded into the ground. Frank could feel the tremors beneath his feet as they passed. He watched them circle at the far end. The starter a mere pencil man among the swirling bulks of flesh.

He knew he should not take Alison's comments to heart. He had been screamed at before, even threatened, spat at by furious clients. Sacked. Dumped. Usually the feeling of failure, shame, passed after twenty-four hours, but not this time. This time her face had remained in his mind. The mouth open. The hatred buried deep in the eyes. Normally by now the unfinished aspects of the case would be forgotten, consigned forever to lost property. But now they itched at his mind. The sense of the man was still there, so that even when he entered an empty room, he felt that presence.

The voice of the commentator ripped through his thoughts. The horses thundered towards him. Swept up, he felt their power, their straining simplicity of desire pass through him. A lone horse cantered back. Its saddle empty. A small colourful bundle unfurled itself further up the track and got to its feet.

He watched the flow of colour as they moved up the hill, and the slight lift as they jumped over the distant fence. Black and white. To race. To win. Right and wrong.

He had sent her the usual letter, signalling the end of the contract. A meagre bill enclosed. He had stamped it, filed it. Case closed. But the photo still sat on his desk. And still he studied the features of that handsome face. It was not his responsibility, he knew that. The horses appeared again. In front, a riderless horse scrambled over the jump. It did not care that it had no direction, no command. It was racing, running, as instinctively as breathing. He saw a flash of animation as it passed, saw the urge to run, to win. The other horses followed it. One fell. One was tired now, trailing off behind the pack. But still moving forwards. The crowd's cheering lifted the horses as they passed.

Was it really wrong to carry on investigating? Or was he just the same as that leading riderless horse? Running because that was what it knew. Not caring that its jockey was crumpled, bright colours on green. Could he accept that he wanted to know for himself? Not for Alison, not for Laura. But simply for his own desire to know that man. The stories twisted round him. Tangling him. He longed for signposts. For a clear sense of right and wrong.

They were approaching the finish now. Their legs stretching towards the post. Their hearts pounding. Sweat flying. But still running. Still winning. The crowd was screaming. Frank craned to see the post. Saw the two horses neck and neck. Saw one push that little bit further, try that little bit harder. The crowd saw. The crowd cheered. Slowly they pulled up. Frank saw the two men nod. Congratulations. Commiserations. By a head said the commentator. Black and white. Simple. You win, you lose.

"Dad!" Annie was beside him, waving a slip of paper. "I won! Look." She pointed at the slip of paper. The winning horse.

"Where did you get the money from?" he asked.

"Oh Dad." A *mêlée* of emotions in a word. "Andrew, of course." She turned away.

Frank fought against the piercings of jealousy. My daughter. Leave her alone. Mine.

"Grow up," said Frank, out loud.

A well-dressed lady looked at him, drawing her tailored jacket closer around her, as if he might be contagious. Frank looked at her and began to laugh.

HUGO WATCHED BENNY ANXIOUSLY as he shambled around the paddock, gleaming in the dappled sunlight. Frank watched his face. Watched his eyes narrow tightly as another horse bounced sideways scarcely missing Benny. Like a father watching a child.

Andrew had given his coat to Annie and was shivering slightly. The horses turned towards them. Hugo fussed protectively over Benny, murmuring to him. Frank watched his hands fondle the horse's muzzle. Watched the jockey pat him. Saw on the groom's face the pang of anxiety. Saw Andrew move Annie as the horse swung round. Protecting. Caring. He wrapped his arm round his daughter's shoulders.

"Come on."

The horses lined up at the start. Frank saw the concern on the faces around him. The love.

Then he saw. Effie. Alison. What had happened that they had lost all care and concern for their children? You may hate your children, be infuriated by them. But they are still yours. You love them, not so much for who they are, but despite who they are. Hugo felt the same about the horses. Frank felt that way about his daughter. Why did Effie not care about her son? What had he done? And what state was Alison in, not to care about her daughter? *Not to care about her daughter?*

All at once implications were screaming in Frank's mind. What had happened? Was she simply horrified by what she'd exposed Laura to? Or couldn't she find the space to love? Was Alison so tied up by hate, so consumed by Kevin, that she had simply forgotten about her daughter?

Annie clutched his arm.

The starter's hand dropped. The field sprang away. Safely over the first fence. The horses had reached the hill on the far side. Andrew's knuckles were white. His fingers wrapped round his binoculars. Frank felt his own muscles tight beneath his skin.

What had caused such devastation that it had obliterated all sense of caring in two people?

A horse fell. The legs tumbling frail against the sky.

"Come on boy, come on," muttered Hugo.

Only two fences left, only four runners still running. Into the final straight. Frank could see the jockey's head nodding stride for stride with the horse. The final fence. One fell, knocking Benny so that he tripped but did not fall. Annie was screaming. Benny came third.

STEAMING IN THE STALLS, the big horse looked proud. Jonny, his jockey's colours still startlingly bold, slid off.

"Thank you," said Frank.

"No problem," said Jonny, ducking away under the rails.

Andrew was beaming. Annie patting the horse. Hugo proud. Frank watched them.

"I have no son." Effie had said. How could you wipe out an entire life. Pretend that it had never been. Could he pretend he had no daughter, no horse? No. Maybe for a day. Not for a lifetime.

ALISON HAD SAT FOR A LONG TIME in the darkening room. *How could he?* she'd thought. How could Frank have lied to her? Made things up? Her hatred, anguish focused on him. But another part of her brain joined in. *Why would Frank lie?* Don't people lie only for some gain, and what would Frank gain by lying about Kevin? Nothing. Black and white. Ergo, he was not lying. But if Frank was not lying, then it meant that Kevin had lied to her. And bells rang in her mind. *My parents died when I was young.* He had said those words, she could hear them so clearly that they seemed like solid figures in the room. Why lie about that? Because it made him seem vulnerable. Like arrows the thoughts struck her. Made him seem unthreatening. Made her want to look after him, comfort him, love him. Manipulative. No, he was not manipulative, he was kind, caring, compassionate. He'd loved her.

But those silent calls. Sorry, wrong number, and him laughing at her concern. That smell upon him. *No.* He wouldn't have cheated on me.

He came through the door and she rising went to kiss him, but he turned away. Upstairs, the sound of the shower. Okay? she'd said. I was sweaty, he'd said, picking her up, swinging her round, kissing her, till all doubt, all those pricklings of unease had been wiped out.

I knew, thought Alison. She slammed her fist down on the table. The pain spun through her bones bringing tears to her eyes. Translating mental pain into physical. She rocked herself, clasping her hand.

No. The smell of scent in his car. Air freshener, he'd said. All those late nights. Waiting. I got tied up. Sorry. Detained. Job took longer. And different scents. Mingling. You'd have done anything to keep him, Frank had said. *No.* Not anything. Maybe. I don't know.

SHE'D GOT FRANK'S LETTER the next day. Stared at the black letters. Ran her finger over his scrawled signature. Remained undecided about him, about his lies, his truths. How could she know?

"Mum."

Alison turned round. Laura looked pale, cold. The puppy sat by her feet.

"What?" said Alison, sharply. Her daughter looked smaller than she remembered her.

"Nothing," said Laura passively. "What's that?" She raised a finger. The skin was white.

"Bloody Frank," said Alison. Two small flushes on her cheeks. "Terminating the contract," she mimicked. "Bloody cheek."

"You mean you're not employing him any more."

"I don't have a choice by the look of it."

"What did you say to him?"

"He'd lied!" snapped Alison. "Lied."

Laura said nothing. Her eyes, oddly blank, rested on her mother.

"What?" said Alison. "Why are you looking at me like that?"

Laura shook her head.

"Don't worry." There was something in her voice. Some endless weariness that registered in Alison's mind.

"Are you ill?"

"Yes," said Laura, looking at her.

"Well go back to bed then." Alison's eyes returned to the letter. She chewed her lip fretfully.

"Mum."

"What?" Exasperation now.

"Nothing."

"Go to bed."

"Frank wouldn't lie," said Laura, turning in the doorway.

"How do you know?"

"He has kind eyes," said Laura, walking away.

Alison watched her go. "Kind eyes," she muttered. "What does she know?" She frowned. "School on Monday!" she shouted up the stairs. A muffled acceptance drifted back down.

MAYBE HE LIED FOR A REASON. Frank. Kevin. Men. She could not think any longer. Could not focus, could not disentangle fact from fiction. Even her memories lied. In her mind she flinched. A raised fist. Lies. Why was her brain against her? She stood up and looked in the mirror. But her mind still swung. Her eyes stared back at her. Crash. The mirror shattered. Shards of glass in her fist and blood beginning to spatter onto the floor. But pain. No pain. She crossed the kitchen. Wrapped her bloody fist in a tea towel and opened a bottle of whiskey.

MARSHA SAT IN HER KITCHEN. The radio chattered in the background, but she could not hear the words. Since Frank's visit she had been unable to paint. Every time she picked up a paintbrush, something inside her shrivelled up and colours seemed to lose their sense. She picked up a pencil and tried to sketch, but vision would not come. Her mind felt blank, yet strangely full. The hours seemed barely to pass. Treacle-like she waded through them. Alison. She must go to her, even as she hated herself for what she must say, she picked up the phone. But her fingers would not press the buttons. Roughly she stood up, shoving the chair out of her way. She picked up the car keys.

THE COTTAGE APPEARED DESERTED when she arrived. An air of neglect encircled the building, as if sealing it off from the outside. Marsha fingered the straggling vine that grew up the back wall. She knocked gently and then pushed open the door. Inside was dim. A light showed from the kitchen. Marsha walked forwards and pushed the door open. Alison sat at the kitchen table. A half-empty bottle of whiskey in front of her and her hand wrapped in a grubby tea towel. She looked up. Her hair fell lank round her face and her eyes looked shrunken.

"My God," said Marsha. She crossed the floor and wrapped her arms around Alison. The stale smell of alcohol mingled with the sickly scent of blood. "What happened Alison, what happened?" Nothing. The figure in her arms did not move, did not respond. Marsha released her and drew up a chair beside her. She took Alison's hands in her own. They were cold.

"Speak to me."

Alison looked at her. She could feel Marsha's hands around her own. Feel the warmth of another human being.

The Kaleidoscope Man 61

"I. He. Frank said. He's lying. No." She pulled her hands away, clasped the bottle and drew it towards her.

"What did Frank say?" asked Marsha.

"He's lying."

"No," said Marsha. "He's not."

"How do you know?"

"Because." Marsha put her head in her hands, rubbed her eyes. To break her idol. To destroy, to rebuild. "Kevin was still sleeping with me while he was living with you." She waited for anger. But there was none and that was oddly worse. Alison looked at the table. Her fingers chasing patterns in the grain.

"Oh." Such a small word.

"I'm sorry," said Marsha, wishing there was a better, bigger word than sorry.

"So Frank wasn't lying."

"Frank wouldn't lie."

"That's what Laura said."

"She's right."

"Oh."

And neither had Marsha been lying, thought Alison. Standing on the doorstep. Her voice. "Don't, Alison, he's bad. Bad news. Please." Pleading. And her own forgotten voice screaming. "Jealous. Just because you're old and past it. Don't lie. Don't lie!" And his arm round her shoulders. His strength holding her. "Piss off Marsha." And the slam of the door. And a coldness in the cottage. And the sight of Marsha's retreating back. Slightly curled. As if protecting her heart, her organs.

"Is Laura alright?" asked Marsha.

"Laura?" Alison's face stared blankly at her. "Yes. She's fine."

Marsha made pasta. Comforting. Nursery food. Simple. Alison ate it. Silently. Laura slept. Marsha found two sleeping pills in the bathroom and gave them to Alison. So that she too could sleep and forget.

"COME ON LAURA, GET UP."

It was Monday. Laura heard her mother's feet on the stairs. Slowly she slid out of bed. She climbed into her school skirt. It felt loose. Her shirt was crinkled. She tied her tie carefully and went downstairs. Marsha was making toast. No one had questioned her presence over the weekend.

"Coffee?" she said as Laura entered the kitchen.

They sat at the kitchen table, the three of them. Alison fiddled with her toast, breaking the crusts into pieces and scattering the crumbs. Laura fed hers to the puppy which sat at her feet.

"Winter's coming," said Marsha, wrapping another cardigan round her shoulders.

"Um." Alison gave up her struggle with the toast and lit a cigarette. The smoke curled round her.

Marsha looked at her watch.

"Right, come on, I'll drive."

They followed her dutifully to the car. Marsha turned the radio on and then up, so that she could sing along to the music. She stopped by the bus stop and half turned in her seat.

"See you later sweetie, have a nice day."

She watched silently as Laura trailed across the forlorn grass to the bus shelter. Other figures bearing the same uniform detached themselves from cars and joined her. They formed a group.

"Why do children always hunt in packs?" asked Marsha as they drove off. "You never see one child alone. Well rarely."

"Laura has lots of friends," replied Alison, lighting another cigarette.

"What?" said Marsha.

Alison blew out, the smoke filling the car.

"Open the window," said Marsha as she swung round a corner. "It's like an opium den in here."

"Sorry," said Alison. She wound the window down. The car filled with cold air.

"I know I smoke," Marsha ploughed on, "but I hate the smell of it in confined spaces. Don't you?"

"Um."

"What time do you finish work?" asked Marsha, moving from discussion to question and answer.

"Five."

"Good." Marsha nodded. "Why don't you put a bit of make-up on?" she suggested kindly. "Here you are." She turned, searching for her bag on the back seat. The car clipped the grass verge and shuddered.

"Watch out," snapped Alison.

Marsha smiled. "Here you are." She handed Alison a make-up bag.

They swung onto the main road that led into town. Marsha glanced sideways. "Look at me," she said. "Much better. You look almost respectable now." A trace of what could have been a grin crossed Alison's face.

"Get a move on, you old fool!" Marsha shook her fist at the driver in front who had just stalled for the second time at the traffic light. Her eyes slipped across again. A fluttering round the edge of Alison's lips. That pleased her.

She drew up in front of the office.

"I'll pick you up at five then," she said.

Alison stood on the steps and watched Marsha fade away.

MARSHA FIDDLED ANXIOUSLY through the day. Alison's eyes rested blankly in her mind. There was a curious deadness about her face. Marsha chewed her tongue and lit a cigarette. As if her brain had shut down, unable to cope with what it must learn. Marsha flicked the ash into the ashtray, her movements harsh and jerky as if her own anxiety had gnawed into her nerves.

Alison had shut her mind. But against what? The future? Did she know she would be unable to cope with what Frank must surely find?

Did I know? thought Marsha. Did I know that he was capable of such devastation? I who pride myself on self-knowledge, clarity of thought. Or was I just as seduced as Alison? But all she could hear was the sound of his laughter, and she only saw that flash of gold as he flung his head back. Was I dreaming? Dream. Did he create a dream? Was it always sunny? Yes. Starkly now she saw the sunshine glinting off his face, but never any rain. Perhaps he had glowed, shone, or simply absorbed the sun so that he too glowed with it?

"Stupid," she said out loud and, laying her cheek on the table, she wept. Not for herself, or for Alison, but for all those who would believe that golden boy.

ALISON WATCHED THE WORDS spread across the page. Her fingers had produced those small shapes of black on white. How wondrous, she thought, tracing their outlines with her fingers. Did I create that? The words had no sense, only the force of habit, so deeply inlaid in her mind, kept her fingers moving over the keyboard. The winter sun began to slant through the window and the soft afternoon light blinded her.

IN A CLASSROOM at the top of an old town house, Laura was touched by the same sunlight. But she curled herself inwards, shutting it out.

"Laura." She could hear the annoyance in her teacher's voice. She looked at the board. The letters swirled, their meaning lost.

"I don't know," she said.

"Look," said the teacher. His hand moved up and down, his gestures large, as if by accentuation he could drum those facts into her mind. But the sound faded away. And the sunlight was touching her now, seeping into the darkest parts of her soul, and she could not escape.

FRANK HURRIED down the corridor. The bangs on his door were becoming louder, more insistent.

Though the weekend had passed with ease, the arrival of Monday had brought a return of the confusion of the previous week. He had talked to Kate about it when she had phoned, but had been fazed by her lack of interest. It's not your problem, she'd kept on saying. Not seeing that it was. Or was it? He no longer knew. The line between professional and personal seemed to have been blurred and he could not find the clarity to redefine it. Something in him knew that he had to delve into that life. But he kept on telling himself, I'm not like that. I remain distanced, detached. What was so different here, that he felt as though he should hurl himself into the ring and confront the lions, or Christians?

He had sat grumpily through the day, fiddling idly, annoying himself, without reaching any peace or any conclusion as to his own state of mind. The ferocious banging on the door roused him from his stupor and he felt his veins pulse as though woken from a heavy sleep.

Marsha stood in the doorway. Her hand raised impatiently to bang on the door again. Her arm fell down to her side and she smiled up at him. There was something in her face that he saw, a sorrow perhaps, but he knew not what.

"Come in," said Frank, stepping aside to let her through the door. He walked towards the kitchen, the sound of her feet on the flagstones following him.

"Coffee." He placed the mug by her hand, reminded sharply of Alison. Her fingers wrapped round the mug.

"Thank you," said Marsha.

They sat in silence for a while. The steam rising upwards from the mugs, two thin trails stretching into the air.

"Very difficult to paint steam," said Marsha gesticulating at the rising turrets.

"Why?" asked Frank.

"It's a very elusive substance, hard to capture and solidify and even if you can solidify it, it then changes, is no longer steam."

"Like describing love."

Marsha looked at him.

"I said you were perceptive," she said. Almost wistfully, he thought.

"No," said Frank. "I was simply illustrating another example of the point that you made. Love is also like vapour, intangible." He flapped his hands vaguely as if dismissing the thought.

"Alison," said Marsha heavily. "May I smoke?" She waved the packet at him. He noted again how strong her gestures were.

"Certainly," he said. "What about Alison?" His tone was light, but under the lightness Marsha felt something sharp, something edged with feeling.

"She's not. She can't." Marsha floundered. The words she tried to grasp spun away.

"Relax," said Frank.

She smiled at him, watched the smoke twist round the end of her cigarette and then spoke.

"She can't believe what you told her. Her mind can't accept it. It's chiselled her out, made her hollow. Do I make sense?" she asked him angrily.

"Yes," he replied soothingly. "When our views of someone break down, it's often hard. For some reason it seems particularly bad with Kevin, as if he were perhaps perfect before."

"Feet of clay," said Marsha.

"Yes. Tough clay." He smiled at her, trying to convey some sense of lightness into the atmosphere. But she did not want to be distracted from her mood.

"I don't think she could cope if you told her any more. And there *is* more isn't there?" Though questioning in tone, her eyes bored out a statement.

"Yes," said Frank simply. "I believe there is more to know. A lot more." He paused. "But how do you know?"

She looked at him, then dropped her eyes. He sensed something curl inside her. Shame. Her fingers moved restlessly across the table top.

"People always say it is possible to put something out of your mind entirely. I never believed them." She gave a harsh, humourless laugh. Still her fingers twitched. "But I did it." Her eyes remained fixed upon the table. He watched her. Something inside of him grew still, waiting.

"Stupid," she said. "Stupid." She looked up at him and shook her head, as if she could wipe out her own wrongdoings.

"What did you block out?" he asked. The twitching obsession to know was tempered by her look of dread, fuelling a certain reluctance in his bones.

She told him. The words crashed between them, spilling out across the table. So that shame and confusion walked hand in hand. They sat in silence. The space between them grew. Frank reached across the gulf. His fingers shook slightly. He took her hand and held it. She watched the meeting of those coarse masculine fingers with her own delicate ones. Inside her something breathed. Something forgotten, wiped out, obliterated, burst into flower. Peace. A strange sensation it seemed. Reminding her of childhood. Dandelion clocks and grass seed.

Inside Frank something sang. "I was right. I was right." Though not with joy, but with triumphant sorrow.

"It will be alright," he said. "It will be alright."

Though whether the words were to soothe her or himself, he did not know.

6

FRANK ATTEMPTED TO STOP the flow of words. "Mrs Gough."

"I said call me Selina," said Mrs Gough pertly.

Frank waited patiently while the words continued to tumble over him. She paused for breath.

"But I'm sitting here, Selina, watching him. Right outside the boozer."

"Oh. Well make sure you do that." She recovered quickly.

"I will," said Frank.

"Good." The line went dead.

Frank peered out of the car window at the pub. The last traces of winter were fading and even in this grubby back street the spring sunshine seemed to have washed the pavements clean, so that the concrete gleamed brightly. Frank changed the radio station and yawned. He was fed up. Fed up with Mrs Gough and certainly fed up with her errant husband, who seemed to frequent only dingy back street pubs. Frank had a couple of times entered the pubs but the wall of sound had shattered as he had entered, leaving only silence. Not ideal places to remain unnoticed. He had now resigned himself to waiting in the car, humming to himself.

Mrs Gough was a large busty woman. His mother would have described her as 'brassy'. Masses of platinum hair, draped with gold jewellery, fluttery hands and chunky legs, ill-supported by tottering heels. He had been tailing Mr Gough for a month now. The door to the pub opened and Mr Gough stepped out onto the pavement, blinking mole-like in the sunshine. He was a diminutive man with rounded shoulders. Frank watched him pull his squashy hat further down his face, before trotting off down the pavement. He waited before starting the engine. In Frank's view the only thing Mr Gough was having an affair with was the bottle.

Frank parked outside the next pub on Mr Gough's route home and sank back down in his seat. A rising irritation caught him unawares, causing him to jerk upright.

"Stuff it," said Frank. He turned on the engine and pulled away.

IN THE OFFICE of Rogers and James, Alison sat slumped in front of her computer. Her fingers moved slowly, almost painfully over the keyboard. *If you refer to clause 3.1 of said document.* The words spread softly across the screen. Despite the sun she wore a thick jumper. Her body had lost all trace of fat, as if her dreams had eaten it away, so that each morning when she awoke she seemed smaller than the day before. And the dreams were coming stronger now, not confining themselves to the dark of the night, when they could pounce unnoticed. Now they sauntered in broad daylight; flagrant in their arrogance. As she turned in her chair, they danced on the edge of her vision. Gently swinging bodies. The rhythmic creak of the ropes. The flattened grass. Their swollen tongues. And at night they walked. *...as referred to in our letter of the 3rd instant,* she typed. And the flavour of the dreams was changing too. A man walking out of the fog. A mountain surrounded by sunlight. Running. Tripping. Falling. Deep wells. High buildings. In her mind she had no balance. Struggling to hold herself steady and always failing, always falling. Stuck. Stranded. Washed up. In the fog a man shouts. A raised fist. A purple bruise. A girl screaming. *We are aiming for completion on the 12th instant.* She had known the dreams would win. But had thought they would take longer, thought she would fight harder. But they seemed to feed off her strength, so that with each day her muscles seemed less resistant to the onslaught of visions. She knew as she had done all those months before that only answers could puncture the dreams, could render them impotent and voiceless. But she could not find the strength to voice the questions.

"DAD!" CALLED ANNIE as she let the front door slam behind her. "Dad!"

"In here!" Frank called back.

"I thought you were tailing that alcoholic," she said, swinging the door open into his office.

"Got bored," he said, grinning.

"Oh Dad."

"You sound like your mother," he said. "What did you want?"

"So exciting," she said, swinging herself onto the edge of his desk. "You know the other school. Our rivals. Well. You'll never guess what happened today." She paused. Her eyes bright.

"Probably not," he said, swinging back on his chair. "But as you're going to tell me, I don't need to guess." She pulled a face at him.

"This girl beat up a boy. Went mad, apparently. Had to take him to hospital. They had ambulances and everything."

"How do you know this?"

"Oh some friend of mine's friend was round there, saw the whole thing. Blood." She emphasised the word so clearly that Frank could see it.

"Yeah," continued Annie, picking at a ladder in her tights. "Laura somebody, I think." She wrinkled her nose up. "Anyway," she carried on.

"Laura?" said Frank and something beat inside him.

"Well some name like that. Doesn't matter. Dad?" She looked at him. He had grown very still. Only his finger moved tracing something on the desk. A circle.

"Dad?" said Annie again.

He looked at her, his eyes sharp against his skin.

The phone rang. He looked at it, picked it up.

"FRANK," SAID ALISON. She leant her forehead against the wall. The headmaster's secretary watched her curiously. "I didn't know who else to call," she said.

"I heard about Laura," said Frank. "Where are you?"

"At the school." She rubbed the soft fabric of her jumper across her face. The secretary was staring openly now.

"I'll be there," he said.

FRANK OPENED THE DOOR and entered the office. The four figures inside turned as he entered and appeared as a photograph, like icicles in their stillness. The headmaster, Frank presumed, sat behind the empty desk. His fingers were stopped in mid movement. His body leant back in the chair to create the illusion of relaxation, though Frank could see the tremor across his shoulders. The man standing behind the headmaster made no attempt to cover his anxiety. His shoulders hunched forwards into crossed arms and his face was screwed up. Alison stood by the window. She looked cold. And in the centre of the room sat Laura. Even among these still people, she seemed stiller, as if her heart had ceased to beat and her blood to flow. Incongruous spots of blood flecked her white shirt. Such a brilliant scarlet against the white that they seemed fake, as if carefully painted there.

"Good afternoon, I'm Frank Hargreaves." Frank stepped forwards, his extended hand shattering the freeze frame. The headmaster stood up.

"Elliot Stone," he said. "Headmaster. And this is my deputy, John Riggs." The tight man nodded briskly, but did not extend his hand in greeting.

"Do sit," gestured the headmaster. "Tea?"

"Please," said Frank. He pulled his chair closer to Laura. "Hi," he said. She looked at him. Then looked away.

"Thank you Vivian," said the headmaster as his secretary placed the tea tray on the table. "That will be all thank you," he continued sternly as she loitered in the doorway, scenting the excitement of another person's disaster.

"Now," said Elliot Stone, placing his china cup carefully on the desk. "Laura, we need you to talk to us." She barely moved, barely breathed. Elliot Stone looked at Frank. "She won't talk," he said.

And Frank could see the desperation in his eyes.

"Should be expelled instantly," said John Riggs sharply.

"John," said Stone.

"Please don't expel her," said Alison, from the window. "I'm sure there is a perfectly good reason." Her hands twisted in the heavy curtains.

"What, for breaking another pupil's jaw?" Riggs spat the words out at her. Frank saw Alison flinch.

"John," said the headmaster again.

"Perhaps I could talk to her," said Frank mildly.

"Why?" said Riggs, with unconcealed anger. "She doesn't need talking to, she needs punishing."

"Has she ever done anything like this before?" asked Frank.

"No," said Riggs.

"Has she ever shown any kind of violence of any kind?"

"No," admitted Riggs grudgingly.

"Were you there when the fight broke out?"

"No."

"Do you know why it started?"

"No."

"Actually," interrupted Elliot Stone, "I do."

"Why?" asked Frank.

"According to some pupils who witnessed it. The boy in question was teasing her, calling her names. Insulting names." The headmaster shifted uncomfortably.

"What names?" asked Frank.

"Frigid," said Stone, staring at the ceiling. "Things like that."

"So," said Frank, "it was really nothing more than a playground scrap that got out of hand, then."

"Playground *scrap*?" said John Riggs. "It took three teachers to pull her off."

"She was provoked," said Frank.

"He's right John," said the headmaster.

"Soft," snapped Riggs. "Give her two years, she'll be knifing old ladies for their chippie money."

"Don't be silly," said Frank.

"She's been under a lot of strain over the last six months. A boy who you obviously know is a bully picks on her. She snaps. I agree she shouldn't have done it. But really,

I do think you are rather building this up into something it isn't. Or," Frank paused, "is it simply because you don't want the public to know the extent of the bullying in your school?"

"We take a very strong line on bullying," flustered the headmaster.

"Strong line on ignoring it, or so I've heard," said Frank. He leant back idly and examined his nails.

There was silence for a moment. Elliot Stone leant forwards.

"Why don't we say two weeks' suspension?"

FRANK REACHED FOR the bottle of whiskey and poured three glasses. The spring sunshine pouring into Alison's kitchen lit up the dust.

"Here you are." Frank pushed two of the glasses across the table. He sipped his own, watching them. Alison fiddled with her hair. Laura slithered off her chair onto the floor and pulled the puppy onto her lap. It seemed to Frank that the intervening months had not happened, that nothing had changed. They were still stuck. He rubbed his forehead with the tips of his fingers.

"How have you been?" he asked.

Alison looked up at him and twisted her mouth. She shrugged and turned her head away.

"You were right," she said. Her eyes looked out of the window down the garden. "I have to know," she said, swinging her head back to face him.

"Dreams?" he asked gently.

She nodded. He saw the tightening through her eyes, the memory of her visions assailing her.

"Laura," said Frank.

She lifted her eyes up to him.

"Would you feel better if I found out why he hanged the dogs?"

Her eyes flicked away. Frank watched her. Her mouth opened as if in speech, then shut. He sighed. Laura looked at him again.

"You have to find out," she said.

"I will," said Frank. He turned to Alison.

"Are you sure this time?"

She nodded.

"I never lie," said Frank. "Understand?"

She looked at him. He saw the fear cross her eyes. Saw her tense against it, drive it out. She nodded.

"Okay," said Frank.

FRANK HAD NOT BEEN IDLE through those winter months. He had had the usual train of simple trailing jobs. Lost children, errant husbands, old friends. But even as his body had passed through those motions, his mind had been absorbed by Kevin. He had been waiting, he now realised, for Alison's call. Somewhere in his subconscious he had expected to hear her voice every time the phone had rung, at every knock on the door. Annie had called him distracted. Kate, with a new, somewhat obnoxious, tone in her voice that did not ring quite true, had called him obsessive. Perhaps, he wondered, as he drove slowly home, you have to reach the bottom before you can find the strength to climb back up. Maybe the strength is only ever at the bottom.

"Dad." Annie was waiting in the hall.

"Hi darling," he said. Then he looked at her. Her crossed arms, the tapping feet, the curled mouth. "What?" He took her by the arm and propelled her down the hall into his office. "What's the matter?"

"Are you having an affair with that girl's mum?"

Frank looked blankly at his daughter. He blinked.

"I beg your pardon?"

She flushed. The colour rising unbecomingly up her neck and fanning out across her cheeks.

"They said. Well, I didn't know. Don't." She stopped.

"Sentence," he said bleakly.

"Mark said." The words tumbled out. "Laura's mum's hunk turned up and sorted out Mr Stone. He said Laura only got two weeks' suspension. They're saying you're Laura's mum's boyfriend." She finished desperately.

Frank sighed. Annie saw something cold appear in his eyes. She longed to backtrack, change the words, walk away.

"I thought I'd warned you about gossip," said Frank, marvelling at the speed of information. "You're as bad as your grandmother," he said, concealing his smile.

"Sorry." She hung her head. He waited. Let her feel the shame.

"Hey," he said, "chin up. I'm glad I still count as a hunk." He laughed. Annie smiled. "Look. Alison didn't know who to call. They've had a hard time those two. They needed support. That's all." He patted her on the shoulder.

"Sorry Dad," said Annie.

He smiled his forgiveness and picked up the phone.

FRANK FLIPPED HIS INDICATOR and joined the string of cars crawling into Nottingham. The roads until then had been reasonably clear, but Frank could feel his impatience mounting. His senses had felt sharper that morning. Each one defined and alive. So that the colours of the cars seemed to fill his vision, their sounds independent, separate in his ears. The smell of their fumes filled his nostrils.

He turned again, streaming round the centre of the city, heading for the suburbs. Filling in the blanks. People, their views, about to flood over him. Spring flashed by. The military daffodils nodded as he passed. The green of the freshly budded leaves belonged to a different colour dimension. And even his own body seemed to grow, pushing against the collar of his shirt.

He turned away from the main flow of traffic and headed out into the leafy roads and endless sleeping houses. Driving slowly now, he consulted his map. The road where he parked was wide, the pavements clean. Frank got out of the car and stretched his arms upwards. His back clicked satisfyingly.

Number fourteen had a dark green door and an old brass knocker. He lifted it. The noise rang through the street. But nothing moved. He waited. His body flicking between impatience and reluctance. There was a scuffling from behind the door and then it opened.

The kitchen was large and airy, carefully designed and clean, almost too clean. They dealt with the formalities of the journey, the problem of congestion. Sam Johnson led him through into the sitting room. Here too the same air of over-cleanliness.

"Nice coffee," said Frank. "Thank you."

"I'm glad you like it," said Sam Johnson. "I buy fresh beans and grind them by hand." He smiled at his own indulgence. "But you didn't come to discuss coffee beans now did you?" His eyebrows remained raised.

"No," said Frank. He pushed his mug to one side. The niceties of convention dismissed. "I wanted to talk to you about Kevin Todd. He was a pupil of yours." Frank's voice floated between statement and question.

"Yes," said Sam Johnson. He stood up and walked to the window, looking down his garden. "Kevin Todd." He turned. "What do you know?" he asked.

Frank told him. But even as he spoke his mind puzzled. That was not the response he had expected. The logical question would have surely been *What do you want to know?* or even a nice plain *Why?* Frank felt Sam Johnson moving around him, sounding him out. His voice ran down, a worn-out record. Sam Johnson was talking.

"Yes. The Youngs. Of course nothing was ever proved. But." The word hung in the air.

"People knew," said Frank.

"Yes," nodded Sam Johnson. "I was the deputy head at the time. Obviously it was not a school matter, but people will talk."

"What was Kevin like?" asked Frank.

"What is anyone like?" replied Sam Johnson. He shrugged. The gesture neat and dismissive, but it struck Frank. It was too planned. Listen for what people don't say, he remembered being told. Sam had turned away from him and was looking out of the window as he spoke. Frank watched his back. "Kevin was a charmer. Everyone loved him. Ian Page, the headmaster, adored him. He wasn't academic, Kevin. But he was a fantastic cricketer. Ian was a cricket fan. In his mind a cricket player could do no wrong." Sam turned back to face Frank and smiled. "Very black and white was Ian. Instant judgements. Which though in themselves are not fatal, they are when combined with a total inability to admit that one is wrong."

"What was he wrong about?" asked Frank. His pen spun across the page. Sam paused. Frank could see him scanning his choices as they unwound before his eyes. A good chess player. Frank felt himself grow wary, poised for any discrepancies.

"There was a scandal," said Sam, eventually. He leant forwards. Frank felt a pang of excitement, but it was flooded by a weariness, as once again he recognised the sense of acting. "Every school has a scandal once in a while. So did we." He paused. "A trainee teacher accused Kevin of persuading her to steal an examination paper for him. You can imagine the field day the local press had when they got hold of that."

"Yes," said Frank, his eyes trained on Sam's face. The ease with which Sam was revealing this tale unnerved him. What else had Kevin done? This story alone was unpleasant, but something loitered behind it, something unsettling.

"Well Ian dealt with it in the manner he thought best."

"You did not agree."

"Ian said Kevin wasn't capable of such an action. He said the teacher was delusional. Mad." Sam frowned. The arguments of the past as clear as the present.

"And you? What did you think?"

"I'm sure he was capable of it. He had this talent for making the unreasonable seem reasonable. He always had admirers, a tight circle of followers. I see no reason why this teacher couldn't have been one of them."

"Did you say this?" asked Frank.

Sam looked at him. He smiled a downturned smile and shook his head.

"Ian did not take kindly to what he called 'school traitors'. He thought that everyone should follow *his* thoughts and actions precisely. I should not be judgemental but he was a fairly stupid man. A dictator. I regret not standing up to him now. But at the time..." Sam turned his hands over and held his palms upwards. "I was younger then. We do not grow truly wise until we are too old to use it, unfortunately."

"Was there anything else that happened?" asked Frank.

"No," said Sam. The word flat against the air. Strange, thought Frank, that a man who has been a headmaster can't lie. Frank looked up at Sam, but he had shifted sideways so that a shadow fell on his face, and Frank couldn't see his eyes. Honest. The word arrived uncalled-for in Frank's mind. This man before him, lying like a child, in faltering stumbling steps, this was an honest man. And Frank knew that, he could feel it. So why was Sam lying? For himself? Or some other person?

"And you don't know anything else about Kevin that could help me?" asked Frank. He made his face open. Appealing to Sam's better nature.

But that better nature had obviously been flattened.

"I'll show you the garden," said Sam, walking away from Frank.

Frank followed, devoid of choice. Sam was talking at him. He was naming flowers and pointing with heavy emphasis at certain plants. The sound built a wall.

"Do you have the name of the trainee teacher?" asked Frank, smashing through Sam's monologue.

"Yes," said Sam, moving away.

"What about Kevin's sister?" asked Frank.

Sam let the flower he had raised drop back down.

"Kathy?"

"Yes."

"Nothing to tell really. Nice girl. Normal. Ordinary. Moved away I think. Got married. Now this is very rare. Look here at the structure of the petals. Most unusual."

Frank ignored the flower trembling in Sam's hand.

"What about Kevin's friends?" he asked. "A tight-knit circle, I believe you said."

"Oh." Sam stepped away. "It's all so long ago," he said. A feeble attempt. Frank thought of how quickly the other names had slipped out of Sam's mouth.

"You remember Kevin," said Frank. A trace of steel slipped along his tone.

"Yes," said Sam bluntly, turning towards Frank.

"Names," asked Frank. The word was black.

Sam looked back at him. Something Frank could not read covered his eyes.

"Adam Waverley. Lives in London, I believe."

"HERE WE ARE," said Alison. She placed a chocolate cake on the kitchen table between Marsha and Laura. "Right, Marsha you be mum." She handed her the knife. Marsha pushed firmly down. The chocolate oozed out of the centre spilling down the sides.

"Did you make this?" asked Marsha incredulously.

Alison nodded proudly. Laura gave a fleeting smile at her mother.

"Wow," said Marsha. Though not at the cake-making, more in general amazement at the effect that Laura's violence had had on Alison.

Marsha had watched Alison closely through the winter. Appearing from time to time, she had cooked for them, filled the freezer, cleaned. Left them alone. She, like Frank, had been waiting for Alison to reach bottom. It was unnerving how quickly she had sprung back up.

"Come on darling," said Alison. "Look I bought you squirty cream to go on it." Marsha watched Laura take the can and squirt the cream onto her plate. She noted the sadness behind Laura's eyes, quickly covered by her desire to please her mother.

"More tea?" said Alison.

Marsha frowned. There was something incongruous about them sitting here, when a few miles away in the local hospital a boy with a broken jaw was sucking mush out of a tube. Marsha shivered. Then held up her cup for more tea.

Alison put her daughter on the sofa, tucked her up, put a video on and then proceeded to settle down and roast a chicken.

"What are you doing?" asked Marsha, unable to bear it any longer.

"Cooking," replied Alison, waving an onion at her.

"But you haven't cooked for six months, you haven't done anything. You've smoked and drunk and bang suddenly you're the perfect housewife. I don't get it." Marsha crashed her fist on the table. Alison looked calmly at her.

"Don't get cross," she said. "It's just that I realised that I hadn't been looking after Laura, I'd been too caught up in my own feelings and that was why she did it. To get my attention." Alison smiled at Marsha and licked the edge of her wooden spoon. "More salt," she said.

"But you don't beat people up to get attention." Marsha was frowning intently at Alison.

"She's still upset about the dogs," said Alison, stirring her gravy.

"Not that upset," snapped Marsha.

"What's wrong Marsha?" asked Alison.

Marsha looked at her. Blankly she shook her head.

"Nothing," she said.

"Good," said Alison, peering at her chicken.

"I must go," said Marsha.

Alison put up a hand in farewell, her eyes concentrated on the chicken.

"LAURA," said Alison softly. "Come on, roast chicken."

She had scrubbed the grubby pine table and it gleamed under the flames of the candles she had stuck in old wine bottles.

"Here we are," said Alison smiling.

"Oh Mum it's lovely," said Laura.

"Here sit down." Alison fussed around, pouring wine, serving, flapping. Laura watched the wax run down the bottles onto the table.

"Cheers," said Alison.

The glasses chinked. The note running flatly across the room. They chewed in silence for a while. The faint noises of cutlery on china filling the room.

"Laura," said Alison. Laura looked up. There was a note of finality in her mother's voice. Completion. "It'll be alright now," she said. "We will be alright. Frank will find out why Kevin hanged the dogs and we will be able to grieve and then move on." Alison reached across the table and took her daughter's hand. It felt cold. "I know we haven't talked about it before and maybe that made it worse. I'm sorry. And I'm sorry I've been no use these last months. I had to do my own grieving. But I feel better now." She smiled at her daughter. "Okay?"

Half-questioning, half-stating, Alison watched Laura. All the love she hadn't felt for the last few months strained at her chest, making her heart pulse against her ribs. She remembered the tiny bundle placed in her arms, the taste of sweat in her hair. The tiny mouth opening. The dark eyes. The intense bunched fists waving. Remembered her walking, hesitantly at first, then more boldly, until she had started to run, to climb. She looked at her daughter now. The line of her jaw, the brightness in her eyes, that half sardonic curl of the lip. A typical teenager.

"Come here," said Alison, holding out her arms. Laura slid hesitantly onto her mother's lap. She laid her head on her mother's shoulder.

"It's okay," said Alison, rocking her. "I'm here now. I'll look after you. I promise."

7

MARSHA ON THE DOORSTEP the previous evening.

"Sorry," she'd said.

Frank led her to the kitchen, sat her down. She'd toyed with her glass, catching the last of the sunlight in its facets, as if she could contain it, keep it, control it.

"Alison," she'd said finally, heavily. The word plummeting downwards.

"What?" Frank had asked.

Marsha looked suddenly old. A sag through her shoulders as if all the forgotten years had scrambled up and pressed her skeleton downwards.

"She's behaving as if nothing happened. Perfect mother. Cooking, cleaning." She'd looked up at him. "Why I should find that more alarming than her previous sloth-like drunkenness, I do not know." She'd put a hand to her forehead. "Her daughter just attacked someone. Violently. And there she is. Perfect family. 'She's upset'," she'd mimicked. She'd turned away crossly. Frank had watched her profile in the dying light. The curve of her mouth, hardening downwards into the thrust of her chin.

"She can't think about it," Frank had said kindly. "She daren't question Laura's behaviour. She's picking up the pieces and pulling them around her. Building a wall."

"For you to break, no doubt." Marsha's voice was flat.

Frank had smiled ruefully.

"Don't pull that one on me," he'd said. "She wants to know why, I'll find out why. When the plate's been broken enough times you throw it away, start again." He'd shrugged.

"Sorry," she'd said with a sudden smile. "That was out of order." She'd paused and it was only then that he heard the fear, the anxiety in her voice. That slight tremble escaping the control of her strength. "I just care."

And she'd opened her hands wide as if embracing that emotion.

"I know," he'd said.

FRANK REMEMBERED an old acquaintance describing the planning that took place in the army. Each minute accounted for and executed according to the given instructions for that time. Even now Frank could remember his astonishment, followed so closely by an understanding that he could never be like that. He simply acted. Then saw what opened up or didn't.

He was heading for Brookes, an investment management company. Late last night, after Marsha had left and Annie had trailed yawning upstairs, he had started to search for Adam Waverley. He appeared to have been quite successful. Frank had studied the photo posted on the firm's website. Trying hard not to pre-judge, he had not liked what he had seen. A handsome face, thanks to regular features and a good dentist, was glazed by arrogance. Even when viewed at eye level the picture appeared to be looking down at him. A harshness in Waverley's eye and a curious twist in his smile. The last flick of the tail of a disappearing snake.

The building was large and square. The front was glass. The name Brookes was etched over the doorway. Frank pushed open the door and walked into the lobby. The carpet was thick. The furniture gleamed. The faint smell of cleaning products could not obliterate the scent of money.

"May I help you?" Large amber eyes looked up at him. A ponytail swung.

Frank flipped his hair so that it fell over his forehead. He smiled sleepily. His blue eyes peeking out from under his hair. He waited. The carefully painted mouth smiled back.

"I need to see Adam Waverley," he said. His eyes brushed her cheek, traced her jawline.

Jolted, she stammered "Do you have an appointment?"

Frank waved his hand dismissively.

"He'll see me," he said.

"I'll just..." She picked up the phone. "Sorry Mr?"

"Hargreaves," said Frank, looking at his watch.

"I'm afraid he is unavailable at the moment," she said.

"Tell him it's about Kevin Todd."

The lift was very smooth. The doors gave a soft musical ting as they disgorged him onto yet another plush carpet. He followed the corridor and knocked.

"Come."

Frank pushed open the door.

Adam Waverley was lounging in his chair. Fingers laced behind his neck. He struck a pose of relaxed confidence. But as he rose to greet Frank, Frank noted a tightness round his eyes. A narrowing, focusing in. He was reminded of a marksman, finger curled around the trigger. Adam Waverley shook his hand firmly but briefly before gesturing Frank to sit down.

Frank settled himself slowly into the chair. As he did, his eyes trailed over Adam Waverley.

Adam crossed his legs so that one foot hung free. The light glinted off the polished shoe. Frank suppressed a spasm of irritation as he noticed the silk shirt, the co-ordinated tie. The suntan. The cufflinks. There was silence. And into that silence Frank felt something seep. Fear.

Seeing that Adam would not take the first move, Frank spoke,

"Thank you for seeing me."

"Not at all," said Adam Waverley. "I'm afraid I can't help you much though." He smiled apologetically.

"You were at school with Kevin Todd," said Frank.

"Long time ago," said Adam, with urbane goodwill.

"Yes," agreed Frank. He paused. "I spoke to Sam Johnson. The deputy head at the time."

Adam nodded tightly.

"He said Kevin had a tight-knit group of friends," continued Frank calmly.

"Boys," laughed Adam.

"Who else was in that group?" asked Frank. His eyes were still and wide open.

"Gosh!" Adam forced a laugh. "I can't say I can remember really." He placed a forefinger on his cheek. A thoughtful pose.

"I suppose not. It was rather long ago," said Frank, dropping his gaze. There was silence. Someone passed down the corridor, speaking into a mobile phone.

"Sam Johnson told me about the trainee teacher who accused Kevin of getting her to steal for him," said Frank idly. "Did you have anything to do with that?" Frank's eyes were pinpricks in his face. Adam was very still. Frank watched his mind work. It was slower than Sam Johnson's.

Adam shrugged finally.

"Can't really remember." He settled for vagueness, which for some reason annoyed Frank more than blatant denial.

"There was a big scandal," said Frank.

"Yes, I do remember something along those lines. The delusional teacher." Adam grinned. The smile genuine. The memory clear cut. Adam caught Frank's gaze. "I had completely forgotten about that," he said. He smiled. His lip curling up.

"Memory is strange," said Frank, letting the words float away from him. "Did Kevin do it?"

"No." Adam shook his head. "Kevin wasn't like that." Adam's voice slowed, but his eyes snapped into focus. "*Why* are you asking about Kevin?"

"Just background research about Nottingham High School," replied Frank, as if he didn't really care. He paused, letting Adam relax. Adam seemed rather slow, thought Frank, as he waited.

"What was he like?" asked Frank.

"Kevin?" Adam looked to Frank for confirmation. Frank inclined his head. "Fun, nice, you know, we were young."

"We?" asked Frank.

"There were others," said Adam slowly. He shook his head and sighed. A bad actor. "Like you said, a group. Can't remember their names though." He shrugged and then smiled good-humouredly before glancing at his watch. Frank ignored him.

"Nice place," he said, gazing round.

"Yes," said Adam, as though he was on safe ground. "It was a very small firm ten years ago."

"Your father's firm?" queried Frank.

"No, no," Adam shook his head. "He was a magistrate." There was a sharp silence. Frank watched Adam flounder.

"Different generation," said Frank, leaning forwards, conveying a sense of collusion. "Different perspective. Over-reactive."

"Yes," agreed Adam, sinking back in relief.

"Disapproving," said Frank. He took a chance. "Disapproving of your friends."

"God yes. Couldn't bear Tom Hutton. Said he didn't trust him one little bit." Adam's voice trailed off. The room seemed to hum. "How amazing," said Adam. "I'd forgotten his name and there it was all along, in here." He tapped his head, grinning at his own bad memory. "Forgetting him. I'll forget my own name soon."

He laughed. The peals fell like lead.

Frank smiled thinly.

"And the others in your group?" asked Frank.

"There were no others," he answered, and there was something so strangely adamant in his tone that, for the first time, Frank believed him.

"Where can I find Tom Hutton?" asked Frank.

Adam looked back at Frank, but soon dropped his eyes. A submissive animal. He pressed a few buttons on his computer and a page popped out of the printer. He handed it to Frank, averting his eyes. Frank pocketed it.

He stood up as if to leave. Behind him he sensed Adam relaxing. Too soon. Frank turned swiftly.

"Did Kevin hang the Youngs' dogs?"

Adam flinched. Knowledge crossed his face. He didn't need to speak. Frank smiled bitterly and extended his hand.

"Well thank you for your time, Mr Waverley."

As Frank left the building he glanced up and even at that distance he could see the tension in the man watching him from the window.

ALISON SANG as she picked flowers. Carefully she placed them in the wicker basket that hung over her arm. She stood upright and surveyed her spoils. Satisfied, she turned back to the house. In the kitchen Laura sat at the table reading.

"How are you feeling darling?" Alison ruffled her hair as she passed. She pulled three vases out from a cupboard and examined them critically for smears.

"Fine thank you Mummy," replied Laura.

Alison hummed as she cut the stalks, tipping her head to examine the effect of scarlet with white. She put one vase on the table and, carrying the other two, made her way upstairs. Laura looked at the flowers. Their colours seemed too bright, too vivid. She pushed them away. Her eyes returned to her book. Black on white.

"Tea?" asked Alison.

"Please," said Laura.

Alison made a pot. She placed it carefully on the table. Laura put down her book and smiled.

"I thought a little walk after lunch might be nice. We could go to the woods."

Laura nodded. She took a biscuit from the plate in front of her. It crunched. Like cracking bones.

FRANK'S EYES WIDENED as he read the document. He ran his hand through his hair. The lady on the desk watched him curiously. He moved his fingers across the paper. It felt grainy. His earlier satisfaction left him. He glanced at his watch.

FRANK TURNED INTO Alison's driveway. He silenced the engine. As he knocked, it began to rain.

"Hello," said Alison. "Do come in." She turned away. He could smell the scent of soap and shampoo. "We're just having tea." He followed her. She cut him a generous slice of cake.

"What a shame it's started to rain," she said, pouring tea.

"Thank you," said Frank. His mouth felt dry, the cake stuck. He sipped the tea. She was telling him about their walk. The words fell round him like crumbs. Laura smiled at her mother. Frank felt weak.

"Can I have a word?" he said to Alison finally.

"Certainly." She smiled expectantly. Frank's eyes slipped to Laura.

"It's okay," said Alison.

Marsha had been right, thought Frank. This cheery Alison chilled him. Smile for the knife.

"Kevin," said Frank. He stopped. Looked at Alison. Behind her eyes the bodies swung. "Kevin's married," said Frank.

There was stillness except for the rain. Alison looked at her nails. Then looked up. Her smile was locked in place.

"Well," she said. "That's interesting."

Laura said nothing.

"Don't you mind?" asked Frank, leaning forwards.

"Not really," said Alison lightly. "What does it matter?"

Frank sat back.

"Good," he nodded to disguise his confusion.

"It's only a piece of paper after all, isn't it?" She laughed. "More tea?"

It was only when Frank went to leave that Alison touched his arm.

"Frank." Her eyes looked troubled for a second.

"Yes." Longing for her to break down and cry.

"Anything else to report?"

Frank looked at her.

"Not as yet," he replied.

They waved to him from the doorway. Their hands moved in unison. Like puppets.

ANNIE WAS COOKING when he arrived home. The smell in the hall made him feel faint, as though the day's events were encased in the scent of food.

"Hi Dad," said Annie smiling. She peered into the saucepan and pulled a face.

"It smells lovely," he said, slumping down into a chair.

"You look knackered," she said, sliding into a chair beside him. "Drink?" She poured two glasses of wine. "Hard day?"

Frank nodded. The wine trickled down his throat, slipped into his stomach. He felt the knot of tension slowly uncurl. He breathed.

"Don't worry," she said. "You'll sort it out. You always do." She smiled at him.

"That's what worries me," he said.

Once in his office he selected music that he knew made him cry and turned the volume up. Seated in his chair, he waited. The music began to fill him, redeem him. It worked its way into the darkness inside and started to banish it. Softly he placed his head on the desk and began to cry for what he must find.

A while later he sat up. The music had left him feeling spent in body, though now his mind was clear. Cleansed. He dragged a piece of paper towards him and began to review his conversation with Adam Waverley.

In Frank's view, the most fascinating insight was that strangely still silence at the mention of his father's profession. Second, was the elaborate pantomime about not remembering Tom Hutton's name.

One at a time, thought Frank. Slow.

Father. Magistrate. Law and order. Law enforcement. If you therefore break the law you act not only against the state but also against your own father. Can I therefore deduce that something illegal took place? Or is that an assumption? How much can you really tell from some half-choked silence? But, argued Frank silently, I felt it then, clearly. Felt the tension ringing in the air.

Waverley. Magistrate. Frank wrote in firm sloping letters on the paper before him. That he put aside: he could deal with that tomorrow.

Now. Tom Hutton. The name had tripped easily off Adam's lips. That was no half-forgotten friend. That was alive. Either the past was that vivid or the past had tangled into the present.

Frank rubbed his eyes. The pieces were falling together now. A picture was emerging and, while Frank fled after that final image, the disquiet caused by Alison grew stronger. The metaphor he had used talking to Marsha of broken plates echoed clearly in his mind. Gradually all he could hear was the sound of crashing china.

FRANK SLEPT BADLY. He dreamt that he was on a mountainside in bright sunshine. But when he turned, there behind him was a patch of mist. In the shape of a person. He turned, running up the mountainside. He could feel his muscles straining through his calves and when he looked down he could see blood running down his legs.

He woke sweating. The early morning light touched the dust on the floorboards. He shook his head, clearing the images from his dream. He slid his bare feet out of the bed and felt the solid comfort of wood on flesh. He padded to the window and looked out upon the stillness.

ALISON HAD NOT SLEPT. She had sat waiting for the first peaks of dawn. Only now there was light did she allow herself to sink under the duvet and shut her eyes.

FRANK LEFT THE HOUSE and began to walk. He wandered mindlessly, hearing only his feet upon the pavement. Gradually as he walked he felt his weariness lift and the strength that he needed to continue came creeping back.

Grinning at the note Annie had left for him in response to his own message, he left the kitchen and entered his office.

The answering machine winked at him.

"Hello, this is Penny White. I got your letter. If you do want to call, please call during the day when my husband is out. Thank you." Carefully Frank checked the number. Another piece tumbled down. Slowly he made a cup of coffee. Aware of his own pulse. The coffee swirled. He dropped the spoon. The noise made him jump. He picked up the phone. Put it down. Straightened the papers on his desk. Finally he picked up the phone and dialled.

IN YORKSHIRE Penny White watched the rain. The letter, hidden for three days, lay before her. The table was scrubbed pine. The paper was cream. The words were black. But the memories were in throbbing colour. The phone rang. She watched it. The smells of the past filled the small kitchen. She picked the phone up.

"HELLO?" The voice was tentative.
"This is Frank Hargreaves."
"Oh." A faint gasp.
"Penny White?"
"Yes?"
"I'm sorry to trouble you."
The sound of breathing.
"I'm sorry to bring up the past, but..." He paused. Gripped the receiver tighter. "But I'd like to know what happened between you and Kevin Todd."
A quiver of breath.
"Penny White?"
"I'm sorry," she said. Then her voice began to tumble.
"I never told anyone. Never mentioned it. Never said his name. His name." Another gasp, as if for breath.
"Sit down," said Frank softly.
A snort, perhaps of laughter.
"I am sitting down."
"Okay," said Frank. "Would you mind telling me what happened?"
"I was a teaching assistant. It was my first job. I had only been at the school a few weeks, when I met him. Kevin. He had blond hair and blue eyes. A week later I bumped into him by chance in a local pub one evening. He told me I was unhappy. He said he could make me happy. He said I had had a difficult life and deserved a better one. We became lovers. He was so strong, yet somewhat defenceless. I wanted to care for him. Look after him. Make him everything he wanted to be. I would have died for him."
"What did you do for him?" asked Frank. Something twisted inside.
"He made it sound so rational." A sob escaped her lips. She smothered it. "He said he wanted to be a doctor. Wanted to help people. Save the world. But..."
Frank chewed his lip. He watched a raindrop roll down the window pane.
"But his chemistry was weak. It was coming up to exam time. He told me he would be the most wonderful doctor. And he seemed so caring, gentle, kind. He told me of

the life we would have. The things we could do together. If he got into medical school. He asked me..." She stopped.

Frank watched another raindrop. His knuckles tightened round his pen.

"He asked me to steal the exam paper for him. Then he could have a quick look. Just to check. Then everything would be perfect. It wasn't cheating he said. It was just to make sure. Just so that everything would be okay. I wanted him so much."

"I'm sorry," said Frank. "I'm so sorry."

"We arranged it all. A foolproof plan. I took the papers to the exam hall. Took one paper out. Slipped it through the window. He passed it back. I returned it. He sat the exam."

The tears ran freely now. Frank watched the rain.

"What went wrong?" he asked, not wanting to know.

"The next day the headmaster called me to his office. He asked me to sit down. He said there had been a serious allegation against me by a pupil. I didn't understand. He said Kevin Todd had said that I had tried to get him to cheat in his chemistry exam."

"I DON'T LIKE to bother you, sir." Kevin shifted in the doorway.

"What's the matter, Kevin?" Mr Page smiled fondly on him.

"Well, I don't like to lay blame, sir. Maybe I'm wrong." Kevin hovered.

"Come on, sit down," said Mr Page kindly. "Tell me."

"It's Miss White, sir. You see." He blushed. "She you know, sir, well likes me."

"Yes Kevin."

"And well you see, she keeps trying to kiss me. Keeping me behind. Not letting me leave. Trying to force me," he hung his head, "to do things."

"Kevin," Mr Page sat up. "This is a very serious allegation."

"I don't want to get her into trouble, sir, I'm sure she meant nothing by it. I wouldn't have said anything. Just ignored it sir, but..." He looked worried. Young.

"Kevin, please tell me what Miss White did." Mr Page was stern.

"But I don't want to get her into trouble, sir."

"Just tell me what happened."

"Well, she, she tried to get me to cheat sir."

"Cheat?"

"In my chemistry exam. She said she could help me. Get me the paper. So I'd do well. I said no. She kept on about it. I thought maybe she was joking, sir. But she kept on. I didn't want to worry you, sir."

"You've done all your exams now Kevin?"

"Yes, sir."

"And you didn't cheat."

"No, sir." Blue eyes, wide open.

"Thank you for telling me this Kevin. It was very brave of you, and you did the right thing, you know." He smiled kindly.

"Yes, sir."

"Well, thank you Kevin. I shall deal with this matter now."

"I didn't want to get her into trouble, sir."

"What happened next?" asked Frank, though he did not really want to know.

Penny's sigh travelled down the phone line, as if she were breathing in his ear.

"Mr Page called me in, asked me if what Kevin had told him was true." She stopped. Frank could hear her embarrassment in the silence.

"What did you say?" asked Frank, peeling her open.

"I lost it," she admitted. And her silence rang with the noise of the past. "I said we were lovers. That we were going to save the world. I told him about medical school." She paused. In the silence Frank could hear the sounds of the street from outside his window: they seemed very far away. Penny was speaking again. The words pressing into his head and making it ache. "Mr Page said that Kevin was only predicted three C's."

"What happened next?" asked Frank. He held his head in his hand.

"He sacked me. On the spot. Said I was delusional, mad."

"What did you do?"

"Nothing. Went home. Lay in bed. Didn't move for two weeks. I applied to train as a nurse in the end." A harsh laugh.

"Did you ever hear from Kevin again?"

"I got a letter a week after the A-level results were published."

"What did it say?"

> Dear Penny,
> Thanks to you I won my bet. £40. Got a B in chemistry.
> Thought you deserved half.
> *Kevin*

"There was a twenty-pound note folded in the letter." Frank could still hear the sliver of tears in her voice. He ran his tongue around his teeth.

"I'm so sorry," he said. "Thank you for telling me."

"It's okay," said Penny.

"Was there anything else that happened?" asked Frank. His voice reluctant. One story was enough.

Penny's breathing altered. Frank's spine straightened into awareness.

"What?" he asked sharply, his voice cutting.

She paused. Frank waited.

"One day," she said. "One of the first days that I had left my house since it all blew up." She stopped. He heard her gulping at the air. "I came home." Her voice had slowed right down now. "All the photographs and pictures in my house had been moved around."

"Oh," said Frank numbly, her fear settling down around him. "How odd."

"Yes," said Penny. "Odd."

The word hovered between them, growing heavy in its simplicity.

"I'm sorry," said Frank. "Goodbye." He put the phone down.

THE RAIN DRIPPED. Frank could hear it tumbling down the gutters. As he had thought, Penny's story was a story in its own right. It bore no relation to the other smoky figures that grappled through Frank's mind. It was but a clue to Kevin. People tended to dismiss lust as a cause for actions, but Frank had always considered this short-sighted. He was sure that, had Kevin been short, fat and bespectacled, Penny would have laughed at such a suggestion. But lust addles the brain, transforms even the very colours before our eyes. Frank groaned. He felt an overwhelming compassion for Penny White and an unusual stab of hatred for Kevin. There was something profoundly disturbing about a man who could destroy someone's life for something as flippant as a bet. As if his actions had no effect on those around him.

But where next? thought Frank. The path he had been following had suddenly widened. The friend. The father. The wife. The step-daughter. Frank had checked up on the wife. She had a daughter. Though Frank was tempted by this route, he felt somehow that the answers lay with the men. The women's stories he could almost guess, but the men? They were not drawn by lust. Or perhaps they were, but Frank did not consider that to be highly probable. So what were they drawn by? What held those men together? The past. The present.

Frank stood up. He would go and see Alison, see if this latest story could shake her out of her shell.

8

ALISON WAS DRESSED in a pretty but demure flowery dress. Her hair was tucked neatly back under an Alice band and only a touch of make-up graced her face. Frank thought nostalgically of the greasy-haired, wild-eyed Alison of the previous months.

"Tea?" she said.

"Thank you," said Frank, longing for whiskey. But none was offered. Laura was placing biscuits on a patterned plate. Frank felt a vein begin to throb in his temple. He massaged it discreetly, waiting for the antagonism to pass. The puppy sat dolefully at his feet watching the falling crumbs.

"How is your lovely daughter?" asked Alison, sipping carefully on her tea.

"Very well thank you," said Frank, frowning at being launched into some sort of social event.

"And your wife?"

"Um, yes," said Frank distractedly.

"Good," said Alison smiling. "I am glad."

Frank looked round in desperation. Laura's eyes rested upon him. Unlike her mother's, they were not glazed. They were resting on Frank coolly.

"The dogs," said Laura harshly.

Her mother made a flapping gesture towards her.

"Not now dear."

"Well when then?" demanded Laura, her voice rising. "Are you just going to sit there drinking tea as though nothing happened? And what are you doing?" She turned on Frank. "Cruising round, chatting to people. You're meant to find things out for God's sake!" She struck blindly with her fists. Hitting out against the pain inside. Frank grabbed her wrists and held them. She slumped. He looked into her eyes.

"I will find out why," he said. "I promise."

She lowered her gaze. Frank felt a churning knot of knowledge in his gut. He looked at her bowed head and briefly touched her shoulder.

"Why don't you take the puppy outside?" he said.

"I'm sorry about that," said Alison with a small smile as her daughter left the room. "She's a little fraught at the moment."

Understatement of the fucking year, thought Frank, anger coming in great gouts. Fraught. Screaming, more like, and you cannot hear.

"No problem," said Frank, tightly snatching his hand away from hers as she made to pat it reassuringly.

There was silence for a moment. The ting of a gently replaced cup on saucer filled the room. Frank cleared his throat. Alison looked up enquiringly.

"I um." Frank stalled. The words sticking in his mouth.

"Yes?" said Alison.

"I spoke to a lady who was involved with Kevin when he was eighteen."

Alison nodded.

"Kevin persuaded her to steal an examination paper for him."

Alison looked up at Frank, her eyes wide.

"He wouldn't do that." She laughed. A silly, girly sound. "Kevin wouldn't cheat. And anyway he had no need." She tossed her head.

Frank clenched his fists. He felt the bones pressing against the skin. Adam Waverley laughed in his mind. The sound grated.

"Why did he have no need?" asked Frank. Each word clean and cold.

"He got three A's." She picked up the teapot.

"He didn't Alison," sighed Frank. "He got one C and in the exam he cheated in, he got a B. He lied Alison. Lied."

She looked blankly at him. Her eyes settled somewhere in the past.

"Oh," she said softly. And even after the word had left her lips they remained in the same shape, so that the word filled the room.

"I'm sorry," said Frank, though his voice carried a tone more of exasperation than compassion, as if his compassion were burnt out.

"I don't see what this has to do with our dogs," said Alison finally. Her voice was sharp.

"Everything and nothing," replied Frank.

"What do you mean?" she frowned.

He shrugged, struggling against his own anger.

"I asked you to find out about the dogs. Not endless unrelated stories from his past." Her tone was rising now.

"But it's all connected," he said. "Everything. Once there are enough stories I will know why he hanged your dogs."

"Okay," she lifted her hand to halt him. Then let it drop as if her muscles had no power to hold it there. "Okay," she repeated.

"I will find out why," said Frank. "I promise you. I just need to dig into his past to find the true answers."

There was silence again.

"More tea?" said Alison.

PETER ROGERS sat in his office. He was meant to be dictating letters. But the absence of Alison had left him feeling unenthused. The receptionist Jo had so far this morning failed in every simple task he had set her and the thought of what a mess she would make of his letters filled him with dread. The intercom buzzed.

Frank climbed up the old stairs. The carpet had worn so that each step appeared to dip in the centre. The walls were papered and old prints of the town hung over the wallpaper. He pushed open the door. Peter Rogers stood up and extended a hand.

"Do sit," he said waving towards the empty chair.

"Thank you for seeing me," said Frank.

Peter Rogers smiled.

"You're Alison's private detective aren't you?" asked Rogers. Frank looked at his face. It was an open, kind face. Concerned yet intrigued.

"Yes," said Frank, slowly, wondering how best to phrase his request.

"I'm terribly worried about her," said Rogers, eager to talk. "She's had such a tough time of it. And she's been very strong really. Have you found out why?" He gestured fumblingly with his hands. Frank saw the distaste on this good man's face at the world that had touched him.

"Not fully," said Frank.

"It's just appalling," said Peter Rogers, his forehead wrinkling.

"I know," said Frank, at once relieved at being able to talk to someone who would admit that it was awful. Someone who seemed to care. Frank began to tell Peter about Sam Johnson, Adam Waverley and his magistrate father.

"I wondered," said Frank carefully. "If you would be able to help me."

"Of course," said Rogers, without thought.

"Could you find out anything about Mr Waverley. Something in the past. To do with his son. I thought maybe as you are in the same field that the questions might come more subtly from you."

"Certainly," said Rogers. "Nottingham, you say?"

Frank nodded.

"Right. I'll make a few calls. Dig a little." Peter Rogers smiled. Filled with relief by this easy-going man who was willing to help, Frank grinned back.

"Thank you," he said.

FRANK FOLDED the piece of paper into the shape of an airplane and threw it across the room. It glided gracefully before banking sharply and smacking into the bookshelf. Frank regarded his stricken plane wearily. He supposed he ought to go and retrieve it. He peered down at his notepad. Among the arrows and apostrophes hovered names. He followed their progress around the page. A snake-like beast, coiled. His finger stopped. Tom Hutton. He rootled around his desk and then sat back in disgust. His eyes drifted across the room and came to rest on his damaged airplane. Even from here, the bold black strokes from Adam Waverley's printer were visible.

"TOM HUTTON?"

"Yeah." The voice sounded as if it had been woken. Frank checked his watch. Eleven o'clock in the morning.

"I'm sorry," said Frank. "Is this inconvenient?"

"No. It's fine," replied the voice grumpily.

"Are you Tom Hutton?" asked Frank again.

"Suppose so," replied Tom Hutton.

Frank laughed.

"Sorry to bother you." Frank began again, launching his attack. "But I wondered if you could help me? I'm a private detective." He spoke the last two words slowly and clearly. The majority of people leapt forward into this statement, Frank had found. He was constantly amazed by people's expectations. On the other end of the phone Tom Hutton laughed.

"I doubt it," he said.

Frank could hear the clicking of a lighter and the suck of air as Tom drew nicotine deep into his lungs. "Do you wear a plastic raincoat with matching hat?" asked Tom. He began to giggle again. Frank sighed. It was perfectly apparent that Tom Hutton was smoking more than just cigarettes.

"No I don't," said Frank sternly. And there must have been something in Frank's voice, for the laughter stopped abruptly.

"Did my dad send you?" asked Tom. The phone vibrated with tension.

"No," said Frank, half confused, half just plain pissed off.

"Are you sure?" asked Tom, paranoia binding him.

"I do know who I'm working for," said Frank icily.

"Of course, of course. Sorry mate." Tom's voice retreated apologetically along the wire. "So," he said. The jokiness crept back into his voice. "Who are you working for?"

Frank couldn't help but warm to him.

"No one you know," said Frank.

"Client confidentiality and all that," agreed Tom.
"Precisely."
"So how can I help?" asked Tom.
"You were at school with Kevin Todd," said Frank.
There was a long silence. The receiver seemed to grow very cold in Frank's hands.
"Tom?" he said into the blankness.
"Yes," said Tom. "I was. A long time ago." The phrase flashed through Frank's mind, it reminded him of Adam Waverley.
"What was he like?" asked Frank.
"Why are you asking about Kevin?" Tom's voice had risen, tightened, into another voice. "How did you get my number?"
"It's okay, Tom," said Frank, his voice dropping to counter the tremors in Tom's. "It's okay. I just want to ask you a few questions, okay?"
"Okay." Tom's voice seemed very small.
"What was Kevin like?"
"Fine."
"Were you good friends?"
"No."
Tom's replies were becoming softer and smaller. Frank could feel him shrinking away through his fingers. Dispersing.
"What happened?" asked Frank.
"Nothing." Tom's voice was barely there now.
"Tom, please tell me," said Frank, his voice barely above a whisper. "Tell me what happened."
"Nothing," said Tom, his voice rising now. "Nothing happened."
"Tom," said Frank.
But there was no reply. Only Frank's voice drifting around the phone lines, lost and displaced.

FRANK LEANT BACK in his chair. He tapped his teeth, his brow wrinkling up. Something had happened. Something to do with Kevin. But what? What action could have such impact as to leave a grown man imploding at the mere mention of another man's name? And, Frank rocked back on his chair, and. Something else had struck him. But what? He grasped in his mind, forgetting the presence of his body, and as his chair toppled softly over, Frank realised. Tom Hutton was in his forties, so why had Frank felt as though he was having a conversation with an eighteen-year-old? Frank's chair completed its backward motion and deposited him firmly on the floor.

THERE WAS A BANGING. Somewhere. Frank wondered if the banging was actually on his skull, as if someone had peeled the skin away to reveal his bones. Even through the haze of his senses, he knew this was unlikely.

"Frank." A sharp voice cutting into him.

He tried to say *Don't. Stop.* But nothing came. Only a swirling vortex.

Frank opened his eyes.

Two fierce green eyes stared back down at him.

"Thank God," said a well-spoken voice.

His vision flickered. His mind jumped.

"Frank."

He smiled weakly.

"Hello Marsha."

"I WAS WAVING AT YOU." Marsha was speaking. Frank was sitting in the kitchen. Annie, who had appeared at some point that Frank could not find in his recollection, was swinging her legs from the worktop.

Marsha gestured with her hands, a fantastic re-enactment. Annie's laughter echoed faintly around Frank's mind. The sound was suddenly turned up.

"And then he just went. Splat!" Marsha's face in animation was beautiful. Her cigarette smoke shrouded her, so that she seemed honoured, blessed, chosen.

I was an escape from his own form of escapism. Marsha's words skated through Frank's mind.

"Marsha," he said into the laughter. "Marsha." His voice must have come out curter than he had intended, for Marsha and Annie stopped, their faces guilt-laden.

"Sorry," said Marsha.

Frank flapped his hand, trying to hold his mind on course before it reared away and danced alone.

"Marsha."

"Yes?"

"Who was the lady before Alison, before you, or maybe even during." The words would not formulate properly, but she must have understood him, for she nodded like a satisfied teacher.

"Jill Bryant," said Marsha.

And Frank's world went black.

HIS HEADACHE must have followed him into the next day. For when he woke, he could feel it, creeping shiftily around the back of his head. Tentatively Frank raised one hand and laid his fingers around his skull. The headache responded, leaping into his hand, a throbbing pulse. Frank groaned. Slowly he made his way downstairs.

Annie was just leaving. She swirled past him in the hall, her youthful energy blazing through him, leaving him feeling weary.

He sat at the kitchen table. Marsha had left him a note. The letters streaked across the page. Alive.

IT WAS A GOOD STREET, a smart street. Frank could feel it in the air, in the graceful trees, and in the discreetly expensive cars clinging to the kerbs like baubles on a Christmas tree. He felt shabby and alone.

"Yes?"

The lady in the doorway was immaculate. Frank swallowed. From the sculptured hair on her head down to the elegant, yet practical polished shoes, passing by a silk shirt and tweed skirt, she had incredible poise. Frank half stepped back. His mind skimmed the memory of the address. He looked past her to the brass door number.

"Um. Jill Bryant?" He asked eventually, desperately.

"Yes."

Frank swore silently, cursing Marsha.

"I wonder if you could help me?" he said.

"What with?" asked Jill Bryant. There appeared to be no curiosity on her face.

"Could I talk to you about Kevin Todd?" Frank waited for the denial, waited for Marsha to be revealed as a liar.

"Kevin." Jill Bryant's face cracked to reveal a smile. "Of course. Do come in."

Frank found himself whisked down a long hall, past endless polished doors, and sat finally on a large cream sofa.

"Dear Kevin," said Jill. She sat very upright with her ankles and knees tucked closely together. "What a sweetie."

Frank stumbled over the mountains in his mind. His tongue seemed swollen and dry. He longed to pant like a dog. Jill was smiling eagerly at him, her eyebrows lifted in anticipation. Frank swallowed again. He felt about fourteen, tongue-tied and useless.

"Um." He floundered. "Did you have, a, um, relationship with Kevin Todd?" He wondered if it was the after-effect of the concussion that was giving him this wallowing feeling, as if nothing was solid.

Jill Bryant tittered. She raised her hand to her mouth.

"Well, yes. What a naughty boy!"

Frank stared back at her. Then it hit him. Jill Bryant was, quite simply, stupid. He breathed. His worry sagging down. He smiled at her, across the flower-patterned carpet.

"How long did this relationship last?" asked Frank.

"About a year. What fun!"

He wondered if she had played hockey at school.

"Why did the relationship end, Mrs Bryant?" asked Frank.

"Oh do call me Jill, there's a dear." Frank nodded, she continued. "Well we had a lot of fun, but he was never going to stay with me. A wrinkly old crone. Was he now?" Jill Bryant winked at him.

"Not a wrinkle in sight," said Frank gallantly. The wallowing sensation had returned, he felt nauseous.

"Aren't you a charmer," she fluttered. Her words trickled over him, making the hairs along his back stand to attention.

"Did you support him?" asked Frank, despite himself.

Jill smiled.

"Of course," she said, as if he were somehow moronic.

"Oh," said Frank. His headache returned with a great clash of cymbals. "Thank you for your time," he said, standing.

"Not at all," she said, her eyes peeking up at him from under her lashes.

At the front door, she smiled at him.

"Has Kevin been a naughty boy?" she asked, her lips dancing.

"You could say that," replied Frank, turning away, forcing himself not to run.

Her laughter followed him along the street, and even when he was safely ensconced in his car, the sound still echoed around him.

IN HIS OFFICE, Frank poured himself a whiskey although it was only eleven o'clock. He shuddered.

"Marsha."

"Oh dear," she said. "Am I in trouble?" She began to laugh.

"I went to see Jill Bryant," he said.

"Isn't she ghastly!" Marsha's laugh turned into gales of hysteria. "Sorry," she said weakly. "You did ask," she finished, a petulant child.

"I know," said Frank. "But Christ alive."

"She's very rich," said Marsha.

"She'd have to be," replied Frank. He sipped thankfully at his whiskey.

IN THE STILLNESS of midday, Frank felt his mind settle. The shadowy figures of those whom he had met circled round him. He watched them, waiting for them to slow down, to evolve their own natural order. Their voices peppered him with words, but they were tangled, just a jumbled, seamless noise. Frank slept.

He woke a couple of hours later. His head felt clearer, though somewhat lighter, which worried him for a moment, as if he had lost his thoughts. But no, they were returning now. But in an orderly fashion. Sam Johnson. Why? Frank waited. The rest of the question caught up. Why did Sam Johnson give him Adam's name and not Tom's and, most of all: What had happened?

"AH YES, HELLO, how are you?" Sam Johnson sounded older on the phone, as if his fragility were presented through his words.

"Very well," said Frank, "and you?"

The pleasantries passed back and forth, like rival tennis players warming up together.

"Why did you give me Adam Waverley's name and not Tom Hutton's?" asked Frank.

"Who?" asked Sam.

And Frank nearly fell for it. But he remembered that quiet evasion in the garden and pulled himself back.

"You know who I mean," said Frank. Anger rising through him.

Sam Johnson sighed.

"Yes."

"Well?" asked Frank. His eyes would not focus. He could feel Sam's shrug travel south down the phone line.

"Adam's tough. Tom's not. I didn't want you giving Tom a hard time."

"Why isn't Tom tough, though?" asked Frank. "What happened?"

"Nothing," said Sam Johnson. "Tom's just not a tough person, some people aren't you know." His tone carried a hint of admonishment.

"What happened?" asked Frank again, but he could hear the desperation creeping into his tone and knew he had lost.

"Nothing happened," said Sam. His voice rich with controlled fury. "Why are you being so inflammatory? Why can't you deal with facts, rather than creating some fiction about something in the past. Nothing happened. Nothing."

Frank might have believed him, had it not been for the last 'nothing'.

"I think he doth protest too much," quoted Frank, towards the silent receiver.

WHILE FRANK SAT pondering the vast gap between knowing something and proving it, Jill Bryant picked up the telephone.

Kevin was lying on a patch of grass, in a deserted lay-by, down some endless dusty lane. He was hovering in that suspended state of rest between waking and sleep. The fast fading memory of the scruffy blonde thighs passed across his vision. He smiled, his handsome features stretching into a catlike grin. Kevin yawned and rolled over onto his back, so that the sun glared down on his face. He moved his arms and yawned again. The slumber was passing, he could feel it slipping away and he hated its passing. His phone rang. Its incessant noise breaking through the muted rumble of passing insects.

"Hello?"

"Kevin, darling." Jill's voice fluttered. Kevin had a momentary recollection of her suspenders and shuddered. His face darkened.

"Jill, my angel, how's tricks?"

Her voice washed over him. Its beguiling rhythms passed unnoticed.

"Kevin, are you listening?" Her voice cut through him. His anger surfaced.

"Not really."

"Oh darling, you are such a tease!"

Thick bitch, he thought.

"I said," continued Jill, unabashed, "that a man came round to see me."

"That's hardly surprising." Kevin's voice was warm, but his face remained impassive.

Jill giggled.

"Anyway," she continued, her voice falling to a muted hush, like a bad detective in a cheap film. "He was asking questions about you."

Kevin sat up. A cloud passed in front of the sun. He scowled up at it.

"Why?" asked Kevin.

"I don't know," said Jill. The undercurrent of excitement still strong.

"What did you tell him?" asked Kevin. The words short and blunt.

"Oh nothing," breathed Jill.

Kevin was silent. His face tightened.

"Oh darling," said Jill, "can I do anything? Do you need anything?" A hint of desperation surfaced. Kevin smiled as he heard her battle it down, out of sight.

Money, he thought, prosaically.

"You," he said warmly, assailed by the memory of his head buried in her matronly breasts. She giggled. "I'll be round in a tick," he said.

He disconnected the call and lay back down. His eyes were tight and his lazy mouth narrow. Questions skittered. He remembered Jill's opulence. Kevin stood up.

IT WAS EVENING. Frank emerged from his office, where he had been watching the last light of the day drift into blackness. The house was very still. Gently he pushed the door into the sitting room open. Annie lay sleeping on the sofa. Her cheeks gently flushed from the warmth of the gas fire, her breathing slow and deliberate. Frank stood for a long while in the doorway watching the gentle rise and fall of her chest and found himself moved beyond thought. It was only then that he began to understand Alison's behaviour towards her situation. The love of your child. The desire to protect, nurture. He quietly shut the door and turned away.

A FEW MILES AWAY Alison mirrored Frank's movements. She too stood in a doorway and watched her sleeping daughter. But her rising emotions were more powerful than his. The desire to protect sprang fast to her throat, so that she swayed from its strength. Alison closed the door and returned downstairs. And it was only then, when she was alone and untouched, that she allowed her guard to drop.

Did you enjoy school, her voice girly in her head.

I enjoyed sex school, he'd mocked her with his eyebrows.

And she'd fallen downwards into him.

Alison pulled her mind back from the brink of that memory and tried to search for others. Words. They must have had conversations; she couldn't remember any silence. But where were they in her memory? She turned furiously searching. But there was nothing. Nothing but a golden fog and a hard body pressed up against hers.

FLAT 2A, GREEN STREET, Edinburgh, typed Frank. He took a sip of coffee and waited for the words to resolve into some form of answer. He swirled the brown liquid in his mug. His mind was strangely blank as though the assault on his senses of the day before had wiped his brain clean. He tipped back in his chair, running his fingers through his hair. The computer gave a small ping announcing its answer. Registered in the name of Mr Robert Hutton. Frank nodded as he read the words. Although this was no breakthrough he felt some sense of satisfaction. His hunch had been correct. But more to the point: the sense of a boy sent away, a sense of distance, pay-off, this was all confirmed by the ownership. Frank chewed his lips. There were many paths now; he pondered the order in which he should travel. He picked up his pen and wrote a string of words. Fourth friend? Wife. Sister. Step-daughter. Fathers – magistrate and policeman. Fenella. Laura? The bodies circled him drawing him downwards. He shut his eyes against the figures that beckoned him.

Precisely, yet almost without thought, he found the website for the *Nottingham Evening News*. With one finger he typed three names. Kevin Todd, Adam Waverley, Tom Hutton. Slowly, almost reluctantly he touched 'search'. Too quickly a headline came into focus. Frank breathed lightly and then let his eyes settle on the black words.

MARK RICHARDS MISSING

The son of local farmer Martin Richards was reported missing yesterday. The Richards family has farmed at Upton for the last five hundred years. Friends of the family said Mark Richards was a popular 18-year-old with his whole life ahead of him. His family have no idea why he might have run away and last night urged him to return home. Mark Richards is pictured here with three close school friends. The four boys were described as "inseparable".

Beside the report was a picture of four boys. Kevin Todd, Adam Waverley, Tom Hutton and Mark Richards.

Frank stood up roughly and put his hand to his chin. The words were moving too quickly around him. He didn't understand. The past crowded him, squashing his very lungs.

"GOSH," said Peter Rogers. "But Bill," he attempted to stem the flow, "it was Waverley I was interested in. A magistrate in Nottingham."

There was a silence on the end of the phone.

"Bill?" said Peter anxiously.

"Waverley," said Bill. "Waverley and Hutton."

"Pardon?"

"Waverley and Hutton." A pause. "Damn old age," cursed Bill roundly.

"Why?" asked Peter.

"Because I can't remember a thing about them. But the names. They fit. Like Bonnie and Clyde. Waverley and Hutton. Bugger."

"Don't worry," said Peter Rogers kindly. But the line was dead.

He replaced his receiver and wrote in his careful sloping hand: *Waverley and Hutton.*

ALISON AND LAURA WALKED slowly along the simple path that curved along the edge of the river. The puppy pounded in front of them, its ears flapping. They walked in silence.

"Are you okay, darling?" asked Alison, her legs swishing against the cotton of her skirt.

"Yes thank you, Mummy," said Laura, her hands clenched deep inside her pockets, out of sight.

"Good." Alison smiled.

Ahead of them, the puppy began to eat the bright yellow primroses that covered the bank.

FRANK STOPPED HIS CAR in Alison's driveway. He was half-regretting his sudden impulse to see her when the front door opened, and a man came out.

Frank got out of his car and straightened up.

"Alright mate?" The man waved his hand in the semblance of an airy handshake. Then wiped his fingers on a rag. "Bloody fridge was playing up. Honestly Ali and her equipment." He laughed and shook his head ruefully.

"Um, yes." Frank's head felt as though it were wrapped in cotton wool.

"They've gone out," said the man knowingly, before continuing his chatter. "You known Ali long?" He rested against Frank's bonnet, as if settling down for a long stay.

"Not really," said Frank.

"Smashing lady," said the man. "I do all little odd jobs for her, you know. Hard to find nowadays, people to do just the little things, you know, leaky taps and that sort. Builders won't touch them, they like big jobs, renovations and extensions. Proper jobs they call them. Now me, though, I like the small jobs. Job satisfaction. You know?" He beamed back at Frank.

"Um, yes," said Frank. His mind would not hold steady, it was heading off track, out of kilter.

"They're good fridges, mind, them. Reliable you know, I mean apart from this incident, solid as a rock. Anyway," he continued, "looks as if someone had been playing silly buggers with it. That'll have been Laura, bet my bottom dollar, if you know what I mean?"

Through his fog, Frank could faintly hear his own voice stretching into hazy agreement. His head nodding, compliant. He dragged himself into the car.

"I best be off," said Frank.

"Right-y-ho then," said the man cheerfully. He slapped the roof of the car with his hand. The noise penetrated like cymbals through Frank's mind. "Mind where you put your foot and all that, nice meeting you."

He was still smiling cheerfully as Frank pulled out of the driveway and headed for home.

DEEP IN THE NIGHT, Frank sat up abruptly in his bed, defying the weight of sleep.

"*Shit*," he said to himself. "That was Kevin."

He was outside, running to his car, before he realised he wasn't dressed. But there was no time to turn back.

The night was dark. His tyres squealed.

"What's wrong?" asked Alison. Sleep hung round her like a sack.

"Kevin," said Frank. "He was here. Today. I'm sure."

Frank hunted. He checked the electrics, the gas, anything he could find.

But there was nothing.

9

It was hot. The air lay sluggishly on the ground. A strange springtime heat wave that seemed to lie ill at ease with itself.

"Hot!" cried Annie, as she came into the kitchen. "And on a weekend!"

Frank grinned and turned round. She danced a little triumphant circle round the kitchen table and poured herself a glass of water.

"Aren't you excited Dad?" She looked at him, so young, so eager. He smiled ruefully back at her. He had barely noticed the heat, had hardly noticed his own body. He stretched his hands out, as if seeing them for the first time. Saw the skin across the backs of his hands, thick, toughened by the years, and yet on turning them over he felt the smoothness of his palms. Hard and soft.

"Dad!"

"Sorry darling," he said. "I'm distracted."

"Really," she said. "I would never have guessed." She giggled, delighted.

"Where are you going?" he asked.

"Alice is driving us to the lake. Go swimming, I guess."

"Alice?"

"My friend, Dad."

My friend. Four friends. One summer. One disappearance.

"What would you do if one of your friends disappeared?" he asked.

Annie looked at him. A frown spread across her forehead.

"What do you mean?" She looked puzzled, worried even.

"Would it change your whole life?"

"I don't know. Dad what's this about?"

"Nothing," he said. Nothing. What happened, Tom? Nothing. Nothing.

"I don't think it would," said Annie finally into the space of silence.

"Would what?"

"Change my life. Not drastically. Maybe if it were to do with me. But otherwise no. I'd be sad. But not forever."

Frank looked at her.

"That's what I thought," he said. But the article hadn't said that the three friends had had anything to do with it.

"Are you okay?" Annie looked at him. He saw the concern in layered traces through her eyes.

He nodded.

"Be careful," he said.

"Dad! I'm just going swimming."

Frank looked at her. Shadows from the future drifted round her shoulders. Men. Frank shook his head.

"Sorry," he said and walked away.

In his office he pressed his thumb and forefinger against the bridge of his nose and felt suddenly old.

In the kitchen Annie frowned at the swinging door. Concern fluttered up, but the sparkling of the sun obliterated it. Her phone rang.

"Great I'll be there." She picked up her bag and ran down the hallway and out into the sunlight.

LAURA LAY IN THE SUN. The puppy lay beside her. Its legs stuck upwards into the clear sky. Alison paused in her cleaning and peered out of the window at her daughter. Wearing a long sleeved top, thought Alison. Teenagers. Honestly. Alison grinned. It seemed to her that the sun was a sign. A sign of new beginnings and a sign of happiness. She vacuumed vigorously, keeping her thoughts sealed safely out of harm's way. The vacuum clanged. She leant down.

"Naughty puppy," she said, "carrying things round again." She threw the razor blade into the bin and turned her attention to the cobwebs.

FRANK SAT IN THE GARDEN and did the crossword. Or rather his eyes skimmed across the clues. He tapped the biro on the chair. The noise was swallowed by the heat. Frank began turning the pages of the newspaper. The action soothed him. Somewhere in the house the doorbell rang. Frank got up, relieved to have some purpose to attend to.

Peter Rogers stood on the doorstep.

"Sorry," he said. He looked ill at ease outside his office. "I should have phoned, but..." He moved his hands in some unreadable gesture.

"I'm so glad you're here," said Frank. "I was bored."

They sat in the garden and commented on the heat for some time.

"I spoke to an old friend of mine," said Rogers. "About Waverley."

"Yes," said Frank, flicking off an ant that was crawling up his leg.

"It was strange," said Peter Rogers. "He couldn't remember anything about Waverley other than when I said Waverley, he replied, Waverley and Hutton. But he can't remember why."

"Waverley and Hutton?" said Frank, sitting up.

"Yes," said Rogers. "He said the names went together like Bonnie and Clyde, but he has no idea why."

"My God," said Frank. "Waverley and Hutton."

"Is that good?" ventured Peter Rogers.

"I don't know," said Frank. He shook his head. Waverley and Hutton. Adam and Tom. Kevin and Mark.

There was silence. Only the noise of a bee sat in the still air.

"Thank you," said Frank. "Thank you very much."

"No problem," said Rogers. "I was pleased to help," he admitted.

"Yes," said Frank. "It is very hard to stand to one side and watch."

"ANDREW," SAID FRANK. "Finally. I've been trying to get hold of you all day."

"Sorry Frank. We went to the Temples' for lunch. You remember them?"

"Yes. Haven't seen them for years."

"You weren't ringing to talk about the Temples, were you?" said Andrew.

"No," agreed Frank. "I want to find an old journalist in Nottingham from the Seventies."

"Right. I'll have a think and ring you back."

"Thanks," said Frank.

He put the phone down. The house seemed very still, as though it were waiting. The phone rang. Frank looked at it and then with a reluctance he could not place he picked it up.

"Dad?" Annie's voice sounded frail.

"Annie, what's happened?"

"I'm fine," she said slowly. "We had a crash. I'm in the hospital."

THE HOSPITAL WAS BUSY. The air full of stumbled cries. Frank ran down the corridor. Annie was sitting on the side of a bed. She was shaking. Frank stopped in the doorway and then she was in his arms. And he held her. And the tremors through her muscles slowed. But still he kept his arms around her. Holding her. Protecting her. He shut his eyes and smoothed her tangled hair, still damp from swimming, with one hand.

"Mr Hargreaves?"

"Yes," he said, still holding her.

"Your daughter is fine. She suffered minor concussion and a few surface wounds."

"Thank you," he said.

Annie detached herself from him reluctantly.

"I'm just going to say goodbye to James," she said.

"Who's James?" asked Frank sharply.

"He was driving," said Annie, walking away.

Frank stood very still. The sounds of the hospital rotated round him. A man. A boy. His daughter. He started walking, following Annie. She went into a ward. She approached a bed. He stumbled across the room towards them.

"Sir? Sir!"

He pushed through the hands that surrounded him.

"Sir!"

He reached the bed.

"Dad?"

"You!" He raised his hand.

He leant against the wall. His hands tangled childlike around his face. He could feel the tears seeping down his fingers. Could taste the salt.

"There, there." An unknown hand rubbed his back. "It's just the shock. It'll pass."

"Sorry," he said finally.

The nurse patted him on the shoulder.

"Don't worry. Here's your daughter."

THEY DROVE SLOWLY HOME without speaking. He walked into the kitchen and poured two glasses of whiskey. He gave one to Annie.

"Were you going to hit him?" asked Annie.

"I don't know," he answered truthfully. "I wasn't thinking. I just. I just."

"You just care," said Annie. "I know."

She wrapped her arms around his waist and put her head against his chest. It felt safe. He put one arm around her and pressed her against his heart as if her presence could still the pain that was spreading through him.

FRANK WOKE LATE. His duvet was undisturbed as if he had not moved, barely breathed, all night. He got up.

Annie lay in her bed, but her eyes were open. He sat gently on the edge of the bed.

"How are you feeling?"

"Tired," she replied, smiling up at him.

"I'll make some coffee," he said.

The heat seemed to have distorted time, so that hours became minutes and only seconds later the sun was sinking and the day had passed.

FRANK TURNED INTO the cul-de-sac and parked. He checked the number again. Fifteen. He climbed out of the car and the heat rose up from the pavement and travelled through his shoes and into the soles of his feet. He moved under the shade of a tree, longing for some trace of a breeze. He rang the bell. Movement somewhere behind the door and the clicking of a dog's claws on the floor. The door swung open. A lady stood in the doorway. Middle-aged. Attractive. Neat shoulder length blonde hair. Only round her eyes did the traces of the years cling tight.

"Phillipa Todd?" asked Frank.

"Yes." A tautness through her voice left the word hanging between them.

"My name is Frank Hargreaves, I'm a private detective." He paused. She moved the door subtly, as if she could hold him out. "I wondered if I could talk to you about Kevin Todd."

She recoiled as if hit. Her skull seemed to leap through the skin. Her mouth snapped shut, her eyes narrowed.

"No," she said.

The slam of the door filled the street. He heard the scrape of a security chain.

"Phillipa," he said to the closed door.

"Go away."

And in her voice something rose. Something beyond the reach of reason. Frank backed away. The street was still quiet. He padded towards his car. A twitch in the corner of his eye made him turn. A net curtain swung. Frank paused and turned back.

Number ten had a metal dolphin door knocker. He raised it and let it fall.

A youngish girl opened the door, holding a baby. The baby was naked except for a nappy. The girl looked at him.

"Sorry to bother you," said Frank.

The girl didn't reply, just waited.

"I wanted to talk to Phillipa next door," he said.

"I saw," said the girl, her lip curling with amusement.

Frank grinned.

"She won't talk to you," said the girl, "not about Kevin. Stephanie will though. Her daughter."

"How did you know I wanted to talk about Kevin?"

"Stands to reason." The girl shrugged her shoulders. The baby raised its fist and waved it at Frank.

"Where do I find Stephanie?" asked Frank. "Next door?"

The girl laughed dryly.

"Not a hope in hell. Flat three in The Mallards."
"Thanks," said Frank.
The girl shrugged again, as if bored by him, and turned away.

THE MALLARDS WAS one of those new complexes on the edge of the town. As if an architect had thrown a load of children's building blocks into the air and watched them fall down. Modernistic, they called it. Frank thought it hideous. He followed the narrow concrete path and entered the building. The lights hummed. He stopped and knocked at number three. A woman passed by with armfuls of shopping and children.

"You looking for Steph?"

"Yes."

"Won't be back till three. Sean stop it!" The small boy was sliding down the railings. He flew off the end and hit the floor. Frank waited for him to cry. But instead he stood up and his face broke into a broad smile.

"Cool."

"Thank you," said Frank to the woman.

She nodded, her attention already fluttering away from him, back to the children, the shopping, the heat.

FRANK SAT ON A BENCH. It was concrete. He lit a cigarette and shifted uncomfortably. His mind seemed strangely blank after the weekend, as if his feet were carrying him in pre-ordained footsteps. He wasn't sure why he was chasing after the women, when he was positive that the story lay with the men. Maybe he needed a break from that breathless feeling that assailed him. That sense of helplessness, that events were moving too fast, too strongly. Frank shook his head. He lit another cigarette and hunched forwards over his knees trying to calm himself, contain himself. He rubbed his face with his hands and sighed.

"Excuse me," said a voice.

He looked up. A young woman stood a little distance from him. Her body was taut and poised.

"I believe you wanted to see me."

Frank stood up.

"Stephanie?" he ventured.

"Yes." Arms hanging by her sides, as if to run.

"I'm Frank Hargreaves, a private detective. I wanted to speak to you about Kevin Todd. Your mother wouldn't see me. The girl next door thought you wouldn't mind speaking to me." He breathed.

"Oh," she let out a breath, her body loosened, she laughed. "Meg rang me, said there was a strange man hanging around looking for me, waiting, she said."

"Well," smiled Frank, "she was right."

"No." She shook her head definitely. "Alice wouldn't have sent you, if you hadn't been okay."

"Alice?"

"Next door to my mum's."

"Oh right."

"She's a funny one, she knows things."

"Oh," said Frank. He wondered whether tracing the men wouldn't have been easier, simpler than the women. Their stories coiled round him.

"You okay?" asked Stephanie.

"Yes, I'm fine." Frank shook his head, fighting against the strands of time.

"Do you want to come inside?"

Frank followed her meekly. Back along the concrete path, through the concrete corridor and into her flat. Frank looked round. The flat was unexpectedly beautiful. Light and airy, it had a grace and elegance so far removed from the brutal exterior that it seemed otherworldly. He looked up. Stephanie was grinning at him.

"It's lovely," he said.

"I know," she replied, as ever delighted by the impact that it had upon people.

"Kevin," she said. And the name jangled in the air.

"Yes," said Frank. "Kevin."

There was stillness and the word lay between them, waiting.

"If you wouldn't mind," said Frank. "I would like to know about Kevin, your mother and you."

Stephanie sat down, curled her feet up under her and looked at Frank.

"Why?" she asked plainly.

Frank looked back at her.

"He hanged a lady's dogs." He saw the recoil in her eyes, and pressed on. "She asked me to investigate. I'm trying to understand him."

"You won't," said Stephanie starkly.

"I can try," replied Frank.

"Um." Stephanie looked at Frank. He watched her weighing him up, and waited. She sighed. "Okay," she said and began.

"My mum met Kevin when I was fifteen. Fifteen. Precocious, teenagerish, unstable. I'm not excusing, just explaining. My mum adored him. Would have lain down and died for him. They got married. I don't know why. Fun I think. He made everything seem fun."

Frank felt something inside him begin to crack. Alison's voice: *We danced.*

Stephanie fiddled with her fingernails. "About two months after they got married, my mother went away for the weekend. It was very hot." Stephanie's voice filled the room, its tone neither harsh, nor sad, just factual. "I was sunbathing. He came out and lay beside me. We talked. He made me laugh. Moaned about my mother. Said she was boring, old fashioned, not like me, I was fun, a goodtime girl, sexy." Stephanie looked at Frank. "Are you judging me?" she said.

"No," said Frank. "No."

"He asked me if I was a virgin. I blushed. Yes, I said. He asked me if I wanted to learn from an older man. One who knew, understood, could teach me, show me." Stephanie stopped. She stood up and went to the window. The screams of playing children floated up into the heavy air. She turned back to Frank. He longed to say something, to stop the story. But it had already been acted out. "Do you smoke?" asked Stephanie. Frank nodded. He held out the packet. She lit one, sucking heavily. She continued.

"He said it would be our secret, from mum. I loved secrets." She drew on her cigarette, her cheeks caving in. Frank watched the smoke.

"We went upstairs."

"Don't," said Frank, shocking himself. "Sorry." He put his fingers up to his face. Stephanie crossed the room and pulled his hands away from his face. She looked into his eyes.

"It's okay," she said softly. "It's not your fault."

He looked at her. She knelt down in front of him, still holding his hands.

"It was incredible," she said. "It was more than sex. It was better than drugs. It was quite startlingly divine and addictive. And the fear of discovery made it more so. Rebellion against my mother gave it another edge. And whenever a doubt arose, or my mind even drifted towards analysing my behaviour, he would touch me. Gone." She let go of one of Frank's wrists and lit another cigarette. She handed him one. "Everywhere. Anywhere. He'd touch me under the table while my mother was there. Fuck me while she was in the bath, on the phone, cooking." Frank turned his head away. "He made it seem so reasonable. He wiped my brain, so that nothing else mattered except him, his taste, his sweat, his strength." Stephanie stood up, letting go of Frank's wrist. She walked back to the window and leant her forehead against the glass.

"I was seventeen. This had been going on for two years. It was a Monday. She was at work. I'd skived school. He hadn't gone to work. We were in the kitchen. I was on the table, he was holding me down. She walked in. We all just froze. Staring. Stuck. He moved first. He slid out of me. Jeans round his ankles. Turned to my mother. Do you want some? he said, thrusting towards her. She threw up. He didn't seem bothered. Pulled up his jeans, wandered out of the kitchen, whistling. I'm there, my skirt round my waist, no knickers. She picks up a knife. I run outside. He comes outside, with a suitcase, puts it in his car. My mother's just standing there with this knife. So long, he says to my mother. Kevin, I say, what about me? I thought you loved me? He looks at me, blankly, as if he's already forgotten who I am. Steph, he says, what you talking about? It was just a bit of fun. Nothing else. Anyway, you weren't that good. And he drives away."

Her voice is monotone now. Frank swallows.

"My mother looks at me and turns away. I go to follow. Don't come near me, she says. She spits at me. I'm there in the street. His spunk still warm on my thighs. Spit on my face. With nothing. Alice rescued me. Looked after me, took me in."

"Did Alice know about the affair?" asked Frank.

"I never told her, but she'd known, all along. She said he was a bad one. She said you could smell it. Evil." Stephanie paused.

"What?" asked Frank.

"I found out I was pregnant."

"Pregnant?"

She nodded.

"What did you do?"

"Alice made me abort it. She said you shouldn't pass on genes like that."

"She was probably right," said Frank.

Stephanie nodded.

"What do you do now?" asked Frank.

"I'm a nurse," she said. "Looking after others. Paying back my debt to humanity. Two lives destroyed, how many do I have to save, to be free?"

"Two," said Frank.

FRANK WENT STRAIGHT to the nearest pub. It was a small, working-man's pub near the flat complex. The air was smoky. He cradled his whiskey in his hands. He watched the light fracture through the liquid and break up, disperse. He looked at his curled fingers, noted the effect of the flesh against the glass. His thoughts came in great gulps, interrupted by periods when his limbs seemed so foreign that he wanted to shed them.

He had thought the women's stories would wash over him, pass him by, act merely as a backdrop for what he knew was the real story. But now. Hurting. Stephanie's fingers curled round his wrists, her voice accepting. Why should that hurt so much? The sheer callousness of it, he supposed. How many more stories were there? Frank did not want to know. Did not want to feel each person's pain, so real that it spat at him and burned like hot fat. He would, he thought, end up puckered, scarred, touched by every word of pain. He got another whiskey. The barman frowned at him as he spilled his change across the bar.

"You alright mate?"

"Fine." Frank nodded, but his voice sounded detached, unfamiliar. He stumbled away. Drinking again, waiting, praying for the whiskey to fill him.

The windows were grimy. But still the sunlight made its way through. The pub became fuller. End of the day. The shouts and laughter, as of small children released from school. But no one came near him. They left him alone. Instinctively. No need to pry. Leave well alone. Children. Annie. Annie. Alone. His thoughts were tumbling now. Faster, chasing one another. And he stood, swaying slightly and found himself on the street.

Car. He found the car. The keys would not fit in the ignition. He squinted, trying to focus. A cold sweat prickling his skin. The engine turned over. The noise shocking him. He drove carefully. Not too slowly, not too quickly. Annie. Annie. Cars jumped out at him. People wandered across the road. He braked. Turned left. Home.

"Annie!" His voice sounded through the house.

"Dad?" She was there in the hall. "Dad are you okay?" Walking towards him now. Worry lines across her forehead.

He reached out, dragged her against him and held her. Safe.

"Dad!" She pushed back off his chest. "Dad. Are you drunk?"

He peered down at her, puzzled.

"Yes," he said, and then, very slowly, he began to laugh.

AFTER HIS HYSTERIA had subsided, he followed Annie to the kitchen. She sat down and frowned.

"What's that?" asked Frank. He pointed to the picture on the table.

Slowly she turned it round towards him. It was a picture of Annie. The glass was smashed.

"I found it in the hall," she said, "when I got home." She paused and looked up at him. "It must have fallen off the wall," she said, but there was doubt in her voice and he could feel her seeking reassurance.

Frank took the picture from her and studied it for a moment. He shook his head.

"No." His voice came out like steel.

He knew how you made the glass shatter in that way.

Someone had ground his heel into it.

10

THE HEAT WAVE HAD TURNED to thunder and rain. The downpour bounced off his car, sealing him in, as he drove. He turned up Alison's lane. He saw the front door open and Alison's head peer out through the hanging rain. He slammed his car door and ran towards the house. Lightning flashed.

"It's raining," said Alison, as she shut the door.

Frank stared at her. But her eyes had taken on a dreamy quality, so that the pupils seemed to be swimming beneath the surface.

"It rained last year," she said, smiling lazily up at Frank.

"Yes, it did," agreed Frank, nodding his head. The hairs on the back of his neck stood very slowly up.

"Do you remember?" said Alison, looking at, but not seeing him.

"Alison!" he said sharply, backing away.

"Do you remember?" She stepped towards him. Her eyes glazed.

He slapped her across the cheek. Hard. The sound spun across the room.

"Frank?" She fingered her cheek. It grew red. He flushed, ashamed.

"Sorry," he said.

Her eyes focused.

"Come on." He put his hand under her elbow and propelled her into the kitchen. He sat her down.

"I thought..." she stammered.

"I know," he said softly. "I know."

"We made love in the rain," she said. Her voice flat.

"I'm sorry," he said.

"Why did he go?" she asked. "Why did he leave me?"

Frank shook his head.

"Do you know?" she asked.

"Almost," he said.
"Why are you here then?"
"I wanted to check on you. Check you were okay."

The kitchen door opened. They looked up. Alison held out her hand to her daughter.

"We're okay, aren't we darling?" She pulled Laura onto her lap. "Aren't we?"

"Yes," said Laura, looking at Frank.

"Frank."

"Andrew, how are you?"

"Good, you?"

Frank told him about Annie and the car crash.

"But of course you'd want to kill the boy driving. She's your daughter. You want to protect her. It's natural. Don't beat yourself up."

"I felt awful."

"That's because you're a good man. Not violent. You just shocked yourself. Is she okay?"

"Yes she's fine. Apart from her deranged father."

"Frank stop it."

"Sorry."

"Right. I've found you a journalist. Billy Mason. Used to work on Fleet Street in the Sixties. Little problem with the bottle. Got sacked. Ended up in Nottingham in the Seventies. Good mind. Nose for a story. Bit eccentric. But good. Works by instinct, when not too pissed. I've got his number. Got a pen?"

"Marsha? It's Frank. How are you?"

"Frank. How lovely. I was just thinking of you."

"I just wondered if you'd keep an eye on Alison."

"Why?"

He told her. Trying to explain about Alison's battle with herself to keep going. How she seemed to be fading between the past and the present. Truth and dreams.

"Maybe the truth is too much," said Marsha.

"I know," said Frank.

"But it's going to get worse, isn't it?" Longing for the answer to be No.

"I'm afraid so," said Frank.

"I'll keep an eye on her," said Marsha.

"Thank you."

NOTTINGHAM. AGAIN. Flat, grey skies above, that seemed to press down on Frank's head as he drove. Maybe, he thought, if the skies lifted, I'd simply drift away. All those thoughts and images would float out of my head and disperse into a million molecules and mingle with the air and be forgotten. The car in front braked abruptly. The red tail lights loomed in Frank's vision. He slammed on his own brakes. His beating heart dragging him back into his body.

Falconer Lane. Frank parked his car. The sound of old jazz music billowed onto the street. Number seventeen. The source of the music. Frank knocked.

"You must be Frank," said the man, swinging the door wide open, so that the music flooded out, filling the street.

"Billy Mason?" Frank extended his hand.

"Dr Livingstone I presume?"

Billy twirled away down the corridor. Taking this as an invitation, Frank followed. The house was small. Books and papers covered the walls, tumbling downwards.

"Sit."

Frank sat. Billy sat opposite, giving Frank the uneasy sensation of interrogation. Billy folded his fingers together and made a steeple. He regarded his creation with a look of satisfaction, before reluctantly tearing his gaze away and fixing it instead upon Frank.

"Thank you for seeing me," said Frank.

"I am but an old man," replied Billy profoundly. He leant back in his chair and held an imaginary saxophone to his lips. His fingers rattled so surely that Frank could almost see the instrument under his hands.

"Um."

Billy smiled. An infinitely slow, stretching smile. He leaned over and flicked the music off. The silence seemed louder.

"Right," said Billy. "Andrew said you wanted to talk to me about the Seventies."

"Yes," said Frank.

"In particular?" Billy raised his eyebrows and turned his palms upwards, as if he were some mafia boss in a bad movie.

"Mark Richards. He disappeared when he was eighteen. The *Nottingham Evening News* covered it, but with remarkably little information."

"Mark Richards." A flash through his eyes. "Well well, you are a little bloodhound aren't you?" He laughed.

"What do you mean?"

Billy shook his head.

"Mark Richards, according to the information handed out by the police, disappeared somewhere along the Upton road. Abduction, possibly. Fair enough. What no one knew was why he was walking along that road. When I started to enquire I was politely told to keep my nose out of police business."

"But his family farmed at Upton, wasn't he just walking home?"

"No." Billy shook his head. "Look." He stood up and crossed the room to the far wall. Humming gently he ran his finger across the files that filled the shelves. "Here we are." He laid the file in front of Frank and pulled out a map. "Here," he pointed, "is the family farm. Here is the school. If he were going to walk, he would walk this way, following the lanes. Not the main road, not two sides of a triangle."

"What about friends? He was walking from a friend's house?"

"Nope." Billy pointed again. "Three red dots. These mark his friends' houses. They are all on the route from the school to the back lanes. And to cap it off, Mark always rode a bicycle. And there was no bicycle found anywhere on the Upton road."

"Oh." Frank frowned. "Do you think he scarpered?"

Billy shrugged.

"No," he said, "but I couldn't tell you why. Just..." He snatched uselessly at the air.

"They had a memorial service," continued Billy. "Remembrance and prayer, they called it. Funeral, I called it. Look."

He swept his hand across the file, and a mass of black and white pictures came into view. Frank picked one up. Kevin. His fingers tightened round the photograph. Kevin, and on one side Adam Waverley and on the other Tom Hutton. And behind them, like fathers, stood three men.

"Who are they?" asked Frank pointing.

"Keith Waverley, Robert Hutton and Samuel Johnson."

"Johnson? As in deputy headmaster of their school at the time?"

"Yes." Billy peered sideways at him. "But also Mark Richards' uncle and, rumour has it, he was shagging Kevin Todd's mother."

And that just slipped his mind when I spoke to him, thought Frank. He rubbed his eyes. The faces were flashing so quickly before him now that their images blurred and he could not see where one stopped and another began.

"The strange thing about that service," said Billy, ignoring Frank, "was the atmosphere. It was uncomfortable, tight, charged."

Waverley and Hutton. Frank tapped his teeth.

"Which one's the father?"

"There." Billy pointed. "And the little sister. Now then what's strange?"

Frank looked at the photo. *Everything*.

"There's no mother."

"Yes. One point. Second answer is..." He did a drum roll.

"They look angry, not sad."

Billy held up his fingers and began to conduct.

"Okay maybe if I were being charitable, I could say they were angry at Mark for running away, but it wasn't that. Theirs was an imploded anger, focused inwards, among themselves. It had nothing to do with the service or the words of hope for Mark's safe return. It was very odd."

"Yes," said Frank, entranced. "What did you do?"

"I dug. I dug. I dug," said Billy, making shovelling motions into the carpet. "But nothing. Not a bloody bean. Brick wall. Brick wall. Brick wall. But I know something wasn't right. I know. You know. You know here." He stuck his finger into Frank's gut. Frank flinched.

"Yes."

"Fishy. Fishy. Fishy. But not a bite on my bait. No bloody hook, line and sinker for me, I can tell you. Poor Billy."

"Did you ever manage to get a look at the police report?"

"Easier to steal the crown jewels boy."

"What did you do?"

"Got drunk," said Billy, rolling the 'r' in drunk and swaying.

Frank grinned.

"What do you think happened?" asked Frank.

Billy rolled his eyes.

"What do you want? Me to do your job for you? You're the bloody dick." He leered at Frank. "Seriously. I don't know. But there was something funny about those three boys. As if they were bonded by hatred rather than friendship. Strange. And the father and the sister. Odd. The whole thing was odd. I'd look at the boys."

"They're men now."

"We're all men now," replied Billy. "Who are you investigating then? Let me guess." He ran his tongue along his teeth. "My money would be on Kevin Todd. I'd say he held the power in that group."

"You're right," said Frank slowly.

"Ping! And the winner is Billy!"

"Hatred," said Frank. "What did you mean by hatred?"

"Maybe that was not the right word. Maybe fear is a better description. As if they held together because they had to, not because they wanted to. And the parents seemed to mirror them. Perhaps for the same reason. But what do I know? I'm just Billy the booze hound. Give me a drink and I'll tell you your fortune." He grinned. "I see riches and glory and women. How about that?"

"That would be lovely," said Frank, but his eyes were cold and still. And his brain was churning. "Do you know if Martin Richards is still alive?"

"I think so," replied Billy. "But where, I don't know."

"And the sister?"

"With the fairies. Flying. Not a clue, my boy. Not a clue."

"I'm confused," said Frank, tracing the outlines of their faces in the photos.

"And rightly so," said Billy.

"Why? Why isn't it clear?"

"The mists of time are always hazy. That's why they are called the mists of time. Did they teach you nothing at school?"

"School. Did this happen before or after the incident with the teacher?"

"Oh that. This was after. This was the end of the school year. Summer."

"I should go," said Frank. Sam Johnson's face rose in his mind. His words. His flowers. He never touched on any of this. Must have known I would find it. But would not help. Or could not help. Or perhaps. He shut his eyes, trying to calm his mind.

"You'll work it out," said Billy. He touched Frank lightly on the sleeve. "You'll do it. I see a light."

"I hope so," said Frank. "I do hope so."

"You must trust," said Billy. He took Frank's hand and held it between his own. "You must have enough faith to step along the path that you think is right and enough humility to turn back should the path be wrong."

"I'll try," said Frank.

"Don't worry," said Billy. "Goodbye."

"Goodbye," said Frank.

And jazz music bellowed onto the street.

FRANK DROVE WITHOUT SIGHT. The past had risen up so strongly that the figures moved across the windscreen blocking out all sense of the road. He found himself driving towards Sam Johnson's street. Just simply driving. Because he could control that. He could control the clutch, the speed, the direction. He could not control the past.

"MR HARGREAVES, what a lovely surprise." Fear snaked upwards. Sam Johnson's voice sounded lonely in the air. Frank pushed at the door, heard the rattle of the security chain.

"Let me in."

"No."

"What happened? Why did Mark Richards disappear? You didn't mention that did you? Didn't mention you were his uncle? Didn't mention you were having it off with Effie Todd? Did you? Didn't think it relevant! What happened?" Frank shoved the door. The security chain held. The pain made him recoil.

"I can't tell you," said Sam Johnson. "I can't."

In his voice, some endless traceless suffering touched Frank, reached through his anger. He put his head in his hands. And at that moment, the sun came out. Frank stood up.

"Mr Johnson," he said.

"Yes?"

"Where would I find Martin Richards?"

"Martin?"

"Yes. Give me a clue. Like before. One clue and I'll work the rest out. It would be simpler if you told me, but you won't. But I will find out. I promise."

"St Peter's nursing home. Old Street, Nottingham," said Sam Johnson. A pause. A breath. "Sorry," he said. "Sorry."

Frank walked away. Under the trees, he watched the leaves begin to flutter in the breeze that had awoken. He leant against the bark. Felt the scratchiness of the trunk. The roughness beneath his palm. Hard and soft. Right and wrong. It was that simple.

He swung into St Peter's. Felt the gravel crunch under his tyres. He parked and climbed out.

"I am looking for a nursing home for my father," he said, clipping his words as if a hurried businessman for whom money was time. "I believe an old friend of his is here, a Mr Martin Richards? Would it be possible to see him briefly?" Expecting the answer Yes.

They obliged. He was ushered into what once would have been a large room. It had been badly split, destroying the original feel of the room and making it seem smaller than it really was.

"He's a little senile," said the nurse softly.

Frank nodded curtly. She scurried away.

"Martin, my name is Frank."

The old man did not move, did not stir. Frank dragged his chair round so he could peer into his eyes. They were moist. Periodically they overflowed and tears unchecked ran down his cheeks.

"Martin," said Frank. "What happened to your son? Mark?"

Nothing. Frank watched his chest rise and fall. The slow gurgle of stifled breath.

"Why did he disappear?"

Martin coughed. Frank could hear the phlegm in his throat.

"What about your daughter, Lucy?"

Martin's head turned slowly, the vertebrae grinding.

"Lucy." His voice was grating, as if seldom used. Harsh.

"Yes Lucy, what happened to Lucy?"

"Lucy," he repeated and his eyes began to stream, as if these were real tears. That name at any rate had made an impression on his dented mind.

"Where is she? Where's Lucy?" Frank leant forwards.

Martin stretched out one slow hand and caught Frank's hand in his. The strength of the old man's grip surprised Frank.

"Lucy," he said. His fingers stroked Frank's hand. Frank could smell him. The scent of age, of decay. Martin lifted his other hand and placed it against Frank's cheek.

"Lucy," he said again. His eyes looked into Frank's but saw his daughter. "Lucy," he said, but his tone was rising now, distress starting to trickle down the cords of his voice. "Lucy." Louder now.

"Martin," said Frank, trying to cut the cords of time.

"Sssh," said Martin. "Sleep now."

Frank felt Martin's grip loosen. He glanced at him. His chest still rose and fell ponderously, but his eyes were shut. Quietly Frank stood up.

"Sleep well," he said softly from the doorway. He shut the door behind him.

The corridor was deserted. Frank walked slowly, thinking. He turned the corner into the main entrance. The girl on the front desk looked up.

"Was everything okay, Mr Hargreaves?" she asked brightly.

"Yes, very good, thank you." He leant on the desk. "His daughter." Frank let the words fall heavily into the emptiness.

"Such a shame." The girl shook her head sorrowfully.

"Yes," said Frank slowly, his voice detached, relaxed. His eyes, which he could not tame, grew brighter.

"It's slipped my mind where..." He put his hand to his mouth and made a puzzled sound.

"St Joseph's in Cornwall I believe," said the girl.

"Yes of course." Frank snapped his fingers. "I knew it was there somewhere—I just couldn't place it. Don't you have days like that?"

HE MADE HIS WAY HOME. Water hung across the motorway, half falling, half rising, thrown up from speeding tyres. Frank watched the red glow in front of him. He reached his house. The rain was falling steadily now. The dull thud of water on the pavement seemed to beat through his blood. He felt cold. Slowly he let himself into the house. From the kitchen came light and the sound of voices and laughter. Frank stood silently in the hallway. He felt detached as though he could not enter that warm room, but must remain shivering and silent in the dark hallway.

"Dad?" And the click of shoes. A shadow darkening the doorway. "Dad, you're soaking! Come on." Annie wrapped her hands round his arm and dragged him towards the kitchen. The pulse of warmth crept through his body and it responded, woke up, began to breathe.

"Christ," said Andrew. "You look awful." He rocked back in the kitchen chair, balancing himself between the sideboard and the table.

"Thanks, nice to see you too," replied Frank, his exasperation half real, surprising himself. "What are you doing here?"

"Charmed indeed," said Andrew.

Annie hovered uneasily on the edge. Aware of something harder than friendship in their tones.

"Shall I get you a drink, Dad?" She spoke through their silence.

"Thank you, darling." He sat down and rotated his head slowly, feeling the grind of bones.

"Don't do that," said Andrew.

"Why not."

"Frank. I only came round because Annie asked me to." Reaching through Frank's anger to the core.

"Why did you ask him round, Annie?"

She turned, a slight flush upon her face.

"Don't interrogate her Frank. She's your daughter. She was worried about you."

"Me?" Frank was surprised.

"Yes you." Andrew let his chair drop back down onto four legs and leant forwards. "Says you've been distracted, worried, reclusive."

Frank looked at Annie.

"Well you have!" she burst out. The child crashing through the facade of the adult. "I've been worried." She chewed her finger anxiously, her eyes watchful.

"Hey." Frank stood up. He put his arms round her. "I'm sorry."

"God," said Andrew, he looked up at Annie. "You didn't mention touchy and emotional into the bargain." He grinned, rocking back on his chair.

"I am sorry." Frank sat back down. "It's just this case. It's..." He shook his head.

"You're an obsessive," said Andrew lightly, shrugging his shoulders. "No problem. It'll pass."

Frank looked at him and then frowned, as if to cover his own discomfort.

"Well I'd best be off," said Andrew. He stood up. His body taller than Frank remembered it. "Bye Frank."

"Bye Andrew."

"Goodbye sweetheart."

Annie just smiled and fluttered her fingers. They heard the click of the front door. A tense silence spread between them. Annie sat down opposite her father.

"Is there something I should know about?" asked Frank. His voice was very still.

"No Dad!"

Frank looked at her coldly.

"I'm going to bed," he said.

IN HIS DREAMS he could not move. He was stuck watching. A baby Annie lay on the grass, gurgling. The sunshine was perfectly bright. The grass glistened very green.

And then at the far edge of the lawn a thing appeared. It was nothing he could place, it was just a thing and it moved very boldly towards her. He knew it was evil. He was trying to scream, trying to run, but he could not. It was closer and closer. It had reached her.

He sat bolt upright. It was morning. He could feel a thin trickle of cold sweat running down his spine. The curtains fluttered gently. He put his hand on his chest and felt his heart beating painfully. He forced himself to breathe slowly, deeply, steadying his pulse. He felt quite weak.

Downstairs Annie was making coffee. Frank padded into the kitchen.

"Morning," he said.

She mumbled something. Her back tight towards him. He frowned at her. Then shrugged his shoulders. He took his coffee into his office. Shut the door. Teenagers, he thought, honestly, always sulking about one thing or the other. He sat in his chair, waiting for the coffee to drag him into the daylight, unblock his mind. He watched people pass on the street. Unaware of those around them they scurried. Always on a mission, always with a sense of where they were going and where they were coming from. But what if they didn't make it? What if they stepped into the road and bam. Gone. No more seeking, searching. Finished. Ended.

"Frank," he groaned out loud. "Stop it."

What was it, he wondered, about the end of a case that made him feel so weary, so resigned to suffering that he could scarcely be bothered to dot the 'i's and cross the 't's? Was it the absence of hope? Was it that, as the confirmation of his suspicions grew clearer, he longed more and more to be wrong?

He had a deep reluctance to get into his car and drive to Cornwall to talk to Lucy Richards. But he must. At some point. Carefully Frank retrieved the daily newspapers from the hall mat and settled down to do the crosswords.

ANNIE SLIPPED OUT of her school yard at break time. No one questioned her and she barely questioned herself. She walked for a while through the town, waiting for the exercise to rid herself of her rage at her father. She lay down under a tree in the park. Andrew. Maybe her father was right to be worried. After all, she admitted, Andrew was old enough to be her father, and her father's friend at that. And yes she liked him. That was true, and she suspected he liked her. But. But nothing happened. He hugged her and that was all. And she didn't like her father's protectiveness, which seemed to have got worse and worse lately. Made her cross again just thinking about it. Maybe I will go out with Andrew, she thought, just to piss him off. But really he was too old, or was he? Annie groaned and sat up.

"Hello," said a man. "What's a pretty girl like you doing all alone?"

"Nothing," replied Annie, looking up at the man. But the sun was behind his head and she could not see his face.

"Wouldn't a bit of company be nice? I don't bite." She could see him tilting his head. Saw a flash of white teeth as he laughed.

"No," she said, suddenly uneasy.

"What do you mean, no?" His voice was very soft and she felt it snake out towards her, drawing her in.

"I like being alone," she said.

"It's dangerous being alone," said the man.

Alone. The word rang out across the empty park.

"I'm meeting someone," she said, trying to keep her voice steady.

"Really. Is he late?"

She flushed.

"No," she said. She heard the gate at the end of the park open, the hinges dried out. She could hear the sound of footsteps along the path. "That's him now," she said, making as if to rise.

"Where do you think you're going?" he asked.

She looked up. He was leaning down towards her. She glanced past him and shouted. No words, just sound.

The man turned. He saw what she had seen. The next moment he was gone.

"You alright miss?" asked the policeman, who had appeared in front of her.

She shook her head mutely, something thudding through her veins.

"Shall I call someone for you?" he asked, concern lapping the edges of his eyes. She nodded.

At last Andrew was sitting her down on a bench. Carefully he wiped the tears from under her eyes. He handed her a cigarette. She took it thankfully. He sat with one arm around her shoulder till he felt her relax. Then, not trusting himself, took it away.

"What happened?" he asked.

She told him.

"I was scared," she admitted, glancing up at his face.

"Of course you were," he said. "What did he look like?"

"I couldn't see his face," she said. "I only saw blond hair."

ALISON DANCED IN HER GARDEN. She moved as if dancing with a man, but there was no music and no man. She twirled away and back. Her hips swung with a sexual energy that had had no release. The frustration eased as she danced. He was almost there. She could feel the tautness of his muscles. The touch of his skin. So alive. Not like other men. She smiled lazily and traced the outline of his lips. Could almost taste the sweat from his body. The scent. Wild. Feral. Base. She swayed again. His hips pressing against hers and the familiar pulse through her groin and the sweetness of anticipation spreading into her gut. Wanting him. Knowing him.

"Kevin," she murmured. "Kevin."

His hands, roughened by work, caressing her, cradling her, holding her down when she struggled. Exciting her. Ragged breath tearing at her throat. The thrill of possession. Pinning her down and slipping inside her. Rocking her. Pain mingling down through her gasping, stifled cries of pleasure. And floating. His breath on her neck. One hand trailing down his back. She gasped out loud.

LAURA LAY IN HER BED. She wondered whether if she stopped all the clocks in the house, all the watches, she could stop time itself. And stay in this cocoon of duvets and absence of thought. She shut her eyes tightly. But the light from outside still crept in.

FRANK HAD COMPLETED the two easy crosswords in the newspapers and was now halfway through the first of the hard ones. He was stuck. He lit another cigarette. Idly he looked out of the window, wondering perhaps whether the answer would be written in the endless shifting clouds. A car stopped outside. Andrew's car. The doors opened. Andrew climbed out, followed by Annie. Annie. With red eyes as if she had been crying. Frank walked slowly into the hall. The front door opened. Frank looked at Andrew. He lifted his fist. But Andrew stepped forwards, into him, grasping his wrists and pulling his hands downwards.

"Stop it," said Andrew sharply.

Annie stood bewildered between the two men and began to cry.

"Annie." Frank forgot Andrew and turned to his daughter. "What happened?" But she turned to Andrew and leant into his chest, her shoulders jerking rhythmically.

Andrew explained. About the man. About the park.

"Blond hair?" repeated Frank. "Blond you say?"

"Yes," said Andrew frowning in puzzlement.

"Wait." Spinning away, across the hall into his office. The photo.

"Did he look like this?" demanded Frank waving the photo at Annie.

"Well hold it still," said Andrew, one hand still gently caressing Annie's back. He snatched the photo with his spare hand and passed it gently to Annie. She moved her eyes over the glossy print.

"Yes, maybe." She turned her head away, back towards Andrew.

"Kevin," said Frank. "I'd forgotten. Kevin. Where is he?"

"Frank," said Andrew sharply. "Your daughter."

"I must go," said Frank. He gestured vaguely and left.

KNOW YOUR ENEMIES. And know where they are, thought Frank. He knew Kevin's registration plate. A fact lodged somewhere in his mind. Waiting.

ANDREW HELD ANNIE and wished he had no morals. Annie felt reassured by the masculine hands wrapped round her slender body. She leant into Andrew, feeling the contour of his muscles through his clothes, feeling his warmth. Andrew kissed her very softly on the top of her head. Smelt the scent of shampoo and felt the softness of newly washed hair.

11

As Frank drove to Cornwall he tried to forget his behaviour of the previous day. In the brutal light of the cool morning his memories made him wince. His had not been the action of a good father, or even a good man.

He had trawled the streets, watching, stopping, watching. The number plate registered clearly on his brain. His senses homed in on the formation of the letters. The gentle curve of the 'c', the angular '4'. Obsession overtakes decency. But that was no excuse.

The cars streamed onto the motorway, jostled for prime place, fought for superiority. Cars the embodiment of people's inner nature. The doormat man, too lacking in strength to push his way into the middle lane, resigned to follow the lorries in their never-ending stream as they drag their way painfully up the slope. The loud brash tailgater looming in his rear-view mirror, causing Frank to swerve sharply into the middle lane. The boom of the exhaust reaching Frank even in the confines of his car.

Which lane am I? thought Frank. Middle lane, occasional scurries of speed into the fast, but always moving back to safety, back to the middle, the beaten track. But he had not been so last night. In circles he had cruised, searching. No thought, just action, fixation. But he had been rewarded.

In the narrow driveway of a small and plain red brick house Kevin's car had sat. Snuggled up by a small practical girly car. Frank had stopped. He had checked the plate. He had loitered quietly on the side of the road. Waited. As the darkness began to streak through the sky, the first shiver of nightfall, he had seen them, returning home. Kevin. And a blonde girl, hanging from his arm, giggling, too high shoes, so that she scuttled and lurched beside him. That girly, somewhat stupid voice had echoed into his memory.

"Mr Rogers will see you now."

Jo. The receptionist. The woman Alison saw every day as she went into work. Kevin and Jo. Frank had watched the expression on Kevin's face. One of no interest in the giggling vision beside him. Undoubtedly a bolt hole if ever he had seen one. A woman who would ask no questions, do his bidding. A place to wait, a place to move from when a better opportunity emerged. Frank had felt a stab of compassion for her, but his decency had checked that. Alison's partner. Taken willingly, into Jo's house, her life, her bed. No questions asked. Any compassion was for her stupidity. Perhaps.

Frank had watched them go into the house. Relief had flooded through, leaving him weak. Relief at placing him. Kevin. Knowing where he lay and where he hid. Frank had watched the door close across the still street. Then he had made his way home. But the house had been empty. The darkness stretching through it, coiled into the corners. He found the note Annie had left him.

Gone to stay at Angie's.

The hurriedly ripped paper. The sprawling letters. He had stared at the note for a while, before crumpling it in his hand. He had chucked it at the bin, but missed.

CORNWALL. Almost as punishment to himself, it seemed, he decided to go to Cornwall. Punishment for obsession, neglect, accusation. He did not want to go to Cornwall. He did not want to speak to Lucy Richards. He did not want to hear her story. His half-formed guesses flickered across his mind, leaving him cold. The truth is better. He remembered his words to Alison. His own convictions. His beliefs. Spat right back at him now. The truth. He grinned ruefully. I could have left well alone, he thought, could have told her to forget, move on, but no. The truth, I said, the truth. So this is all my doing, my fault. He laughed, surprising himself. Does everything come down to blame, accusation?

ST JOSEPH'S RESTED ON THE EDGE of the Cornish coast. It stood alone, some distance from St Ives. It was an austere building, built, Frank suspected, by a strong-minded individual. Creepily Gothic even in the sunshine with the crashing waves and salty spray. It must be a tiring place. Strange location for a mental hospital. For surely the sea would threaten and send one spinning back into one's own private hell. But who else would live here? Not a family. It had probably been cheap to buy, reasoned Frank, looking up reluctantly at the pointed, narrow windows. He walked slowly inside. The atmosphere took him by surprise. Rather than the gloom-laden dusty feel he had expected, the air was light and clean. Distant conversations scattered through the air, filling the vast hall with the sound of merriment.

"I rang," said Frank. For once not lying.

"Yes, Mr Hargreaves?"

He smiled. The nurse beamed back at him.

"Here to see Lucy Richards in connection with the disappearance of her brother?"

He agreed. His stomach churned uncomfortably and the worry must have shown on his face, for the nurse patted his hand kindly.

"It's okay," she said. "She won't bite."

"No." Frank laughed.

"Follow me." She turned away and walked briskly across the hallway to the main staircase. Frank followed, concentrating on the movement of her hips, her ankles, anything but his destination. The nurse stopped abruptly, so that Frank walking too close behind collided with her. He apologised. The nurse giggled. A tempting sound in this house of the ill. She knocked cleanly on the door.

"Come in."

"Lucy. This is the gentleman who rang about coming to see you. Mr Frank Hargreaves."

"How do you do?" said Lucy Richards extending her hand.

Wrong-footed, Frank gulped. As if he had fallen into some Victorian family saga.

"How do you do," he replied after a moment's hesitation. He took her hand. Her grip was surprisingly firm, coherent.

The door closed. Frank looked round. The nurse had gone. Frank looked back at Lucy Richards. Where to begin? Where to end? And the middle?

"Why don't you sit down?" said Lucy, gesturing to a chair. She sat. He obeyed. He looked at her. She was quite strikingly beautiful. Small porcelain features. Bright blue eyes and silky blonde hair. She smiled at him, her eyes flashing the sun's reflection, dazzling him. She put her head on one side and regarded him, eyebrows raised, questioning.

"Um." Speak, thought Frank, speak. "This is very nice," he said lamely, his hand sweeping the room.

"Thank you," she said. "I decorated it myself. Long-term residents are encouraged to treat their rooms as their own." Her voice had a peculiar quality, almost robotic.

"How long have you been here?" asked Frank.

"Since I was fifteen."

"Oh." He looked at her. She seemed to have barely aged, as if the lack of contact with the outside world had prevented her growing old.

"I like it," she said simply. She linked her fingers and pushed her hands away from herself. A curious gesture.

"Good," he said.

"You wanted to speak about my brother, I believe?"

"Yes. If you don't mind," said Frank, blushing, stammering. A teenager on his first date.

"What do you want to know?"

Frank looked at her. He licked his lips, cornered, nervous.

"Your brother, Mark." Frank stopped.

"Yes," she nodded. He wondered if he imagined the hint of encouragement in her eyes.

"He disappeared, didn't he, presumed dead." Frank regretted the word even as it left his lips. So flat, so final.

But Lucy didn't seem to mind the word. He wondered if it had touched her, or simply bounced away, forgotten. She nodded.

"Why?" asked Frank. The question leaping from his mouth.

Lucy stared back at him.

"Sorry," said Frank. The desire for the truth burned his mouth. She must have seen some glimmer of the compulsion in his eyes, for she leant towards him.

"Why do you want to know?" she asked.

Frank forced himself to sit back in his chair. *Be a professional*, he told himself.

"I'm investigating Kevin Todd," he said. Perfect. But emotion thrust him forward on his chair, straining towards her. "Something happened," he said. "Something. I know."

He flopped back into his chair, spent, and looked away from her calm gaze. He was washed up, wiped out, fucked up. He stared at the ceiling and felt nothing.

But her voice reached out to him.

"Mr Hargreaves," said Lucy.

Slowly, almost reluctantly he lowered his gaze to meet hers.

"Frank," he said automatically.

"I'll tell you what happened," she said. The words fell softly.

"Why me?" asked Frank, understanding in an instant that this was a truth that had been left hidden all these years.

"Because," she said, shrugging her shoulders. She paused waiting for the words. "Because you want to know. Not to heal me, nor to win any points, but because you believe in right and wrong. Because I knew I'd have to tell someone in the end."

She looked at him. Frank shifted in his chair. He wasn't sure he wanted to receive her offering, but it was too late. Her mouth was opening and the past was spilling in pools into the air between them.

"I ALWAYS WANTED TO PLAY with my brother. But he wouldn't let me. Said I was too young. I was eight. He was sixteen. A world apart. I envied his friends. They used to go to this old shed after school, at the bottom of the garden. Their den. I followed them in one day. Said please let me play. No, Mark shouted. Wait, said Kevin. Why shouldn't she play with us, or we with her? He laughed."

Frank put his head in his hands. Something bigger than sorrow, larger than grief rose up. He held his head. But she kept on speaking.

"Kevin told me to take my pants off and lie down. I did." Lucy reached out and lifted Frank's head. She looked into his eyes. He flinched backwards.

"He stuck his fingers inside me. Then undid his trousers. I remember being fascinated by him. I watched. He masturbated. The others joined in. Kevin told me it was our secret, our little game. His eyes glinted." Lucy looked at Frank. "I didn't know it was wrong."

"No," said Frank. "No, you wouldn't." Inside him something wept.

"As time went on they grew bolder. The games became more serious. More real. They began to rape me when I was nine. I asked them not to. But they wouldn't listen. They wouldn't stop."

Frank stood up and went to the window. The sea was still there. The waves still followed their rhythmic flow, unaffected, untouched. Pure. Clean. Innocent. Lucy continued.

"They became rougher. More violent." She remembered the muddy floor of the hut. Ripping, searing pain. The taste of the earth. Salty tears. The heavy panting of the men above her. The ache of desolation. Shame.

Frank looked up. But her face was calm, serene. The words that slipped out so at odds with her serenity that they seemed even more brutal.

"I was ten the day my father walked in. Ten. Strapped to a chair. Kevin inside me. Mark forcing my mouth open. Adam laughing. Tom half excited, half repulsed in the corner. The door opened. My father stood there. Stillness. Silence. Except for my tears." Lucy stopped. Frank looked at her.

"What did he do?" asked Frank.

"He cried," said Lucy. "He cried. I had never seen an adult cry. Then walked inside the shed. He untied me. Took the rope and tied Mark's hands behind his back. He told me to go to my room. I thought I was in trouble. From my room I could see the other three running. But I never saw Mark again. Never. I couldn't speak to my father. I stayed in my room. Five years we never spoke about it. Never. He found me hanging in the hallway when I was fifteen. He sent me here. Committed. Mad. I think he just couldn't bear it. Think whenever he looked at me he saw me tied to a chair, naked, ten years old. Couldn't face it, or me."

Frank pressed his fingers into his skull. His eyes wet. His jaw ached.

"I'm sorry," he said. The word so small in the face of such actions. Lucy still sat in her chair. Her face was blank. Emotions cut off when she was ten. Trapped. "Does anyone else know?" He watched her. Watched her stillness, her composure.

"No," she said. "Only you and my father."

"Oh." Frank shut his eyes. Kevin's smile glinted cruelly through him. "I want," he said looking at her, "to go to the police. Would you mind?"

She shook her head.

"Why?" she asked.
"To protect."
She nodded.
"He shouldn't be out there walking around."
"Kevin?" she asked.
"Yes. He sounds like the instigator."
"He was," she said simply.

FRANK SAT ON THE EDGE of the cliff. He floated above the sea, above the waves. The road before him was paved. He felt no anger. The sea murmured, and it sounded like the cries of children.

12

Frank woke. In his mind even as he surfaced from the ties of sleep, Alison's face loomed. Her words printed clearly in his mind. *I want to know him.*

Frank sat up. He sighed. He swung his legs out of the bed and slid his feet onto the floor. He dressed slowly, deliberately, giving each action his undivided attention as if that in itself could prevent the day progressing. He made his way downstairs. Outside, the birds sang. A sound of such exquisite beauty that he stopped, overwhelmed. He forced himself onwards. He made coffee and cleaned the sink. Rubbing away until his muscles ached. And the pain soared from his shoulders cleansing him. He clung weakly to the sideboard, slowly sipping on his coffee.

"Morning," said Annie, stumbling hazily through the doorway. They sat in companionable silence. The steam rose from their mugs and then disappeared out of sight. If only our problems vanished so easily, thought Frank. Bang. Gone.

He drove carefully, nerves on edge. Adrenalin pulsed, pulled back only by despair. His blood punched through his veins one second, fell into a slow sluggish trickle the next. He pushed his hair back off his forehead and discovered it was drenched with sweat. He wound down the window. The breeze cooled him, till he shivered.

"Hello Frank," said Alison, as she opened the door. She looked up at him. His hair was plastered to his forehead and sweat glistened along his top lip like pearls.

"Are you alright?" she asked tenderly, motherly. She stretched out a worried hand.

"Fine," said Frank. He smiled at her but saw only Lucy.

"Come in," said Alison, stepping aside.

They sat in the kitchen. She made tea. The shivers left his body and he felt only tired and sad.

Laura entered silently, her feet barely making a dent upon the carpet as she walked. She nodded briefly to Frank and sank to the floor. Her long, loose limbs tangled round the puppy. A mass of legs.

"Alison," said Frank. And the word grated against his throat. He took a sip of tea. "Alison."

"Yes," she said. Her eyes looked straight at him, into him. He swallowed.

"You said you wanted to know him," said Frank. His eyes dropped to the table. He lifted his hand and massaged the back of his neck. "You wanted to know," he said again and even in his own ears he sounded pleading.

"What?" asked Alison, sitting very still. Only the slight shake of her hand revealing her tension.

He told her.

The words tumbled downwards and spilled sideways. They fell between them. Alison said nothing. Frank looked up at her. Then he looked away. They sat in the stillness and only the words spoke.

FRANK STOPPED OUTSIDE the police station. He looked up. The windows seemed bleak and watchful from down below. He waited. His head felt light and a gentle ringing had started through his ears. As he watched, the front door swung open and two uniformed officers walked out onto the street. He watched the girl laugh at some comment the man had made. He watched her throw her head back, saw the line of her throat stretching so vulnerably in the clear air. She tossed her hair and smiled sideways at the man. Delighting in his company. To Frank it seemed as though he could see the sexual energy dancing between them. Small waves of pink and purple. Lucy. That was what should have been.

Frank walked into the police station.

The officer at the front desk looked up.

"May I help you?"

"Could I see DI Miller, please."

"Your name?"

"Frank Hargreaves."

The officer nodded towards the plastic chairs that hugged the walls. Frank sat down. His eyes slipped over the posters that covered the walls, could not take in their images. He stared at the floor. Watched his neatly-clad feet rest upon the scuffed ground.

"FRANK, long time no see."

They shook hands.

"I've been busy," replied Frank.

Miller grimaced.

"I'd guessed that, else you wouldn't be here." He folded his newspaper and dropped it on the floor. He tapped the pen against his teeth. The thuggish eyes half-hidden by heavy brows.

"What's up Frank?"

"I don't know," replied Frank, overwhelmed by the words that fought to tell their story.

"Frank," snapped Miller.

Frank flinched.

"The beginning," murmured Frank. "Right. Last autumn I was engaged by a lady to investigate why her ex-boyfriend had hanged their family dogs. The boyfriend's name is Kevin Todd. I investigated his past and this is what I found."

Frank's voice rose and fell as he told Miller about Kevin's past, about Penny, Stephanie, Marsha, Alison and finally about Lucy. Miller listened and Frank watched his face. Frank could see the slight tightening through the corners of his eyes. He saw a subtle shimmer through his cheek, heard his breathing change. These were such small adjustments that only one who knew him well could have discerned a difference.

"Right," said Miller finally.

They sat in silence and the sounds of the station trickled into the small room. Miller sat totally still, as if needing to allow what he had heard to filter from his ears to his body and hence into his very self.

"Okay. We can arrest him for the abuse of Lucy Richards," said Miller. "For starters. I think we'll need a little more to make it stick, though. What are your thoughts?"

"Waverley and Hutton," replied Frank. "Sam Johnson. There is a second story connected to Lucy Richards, one that I've only touched on."

Miller chewed on the end of his pen and nodded. He drew a box on his notepad and a smaller box inside.

"Also," said Frank. "I think you should talk to Laura."

ALISON CAREFULLY SIFTED flour into a mixing bowl. She began to stir. She watched as the ingredients began to mingle.

"Chocolate or coffee, darling?"

"Chocolate please," replied Laura.

Alison hummed as she poured the mixture into two cake tins. She popped them into the oven and began to wash up. The sun fractured through the crystal making the room glow. The smell of baking cakes began to drift enticingly around the room.

"Are you okay, darling?" asked Alison, wiping her hands dry on a clean towel.

"Yes thank you Mummy," replied Laura.

"FRANK!" ALISON'S VOICE on the phone. The panic came thudding down the line making Frank wince. He gripped the receiver, but the sweat that had formed in his palm made it slippery.

"The police want to question Laura. Why? Why Frank?"

He shut his eyes and pressed his forehead against the wall.

"Would you like me to come with you?" asked Frank, skirting the question.

"Please." Her voice a breath now. A snag in the wind. A touch.

THEY HAD SENT AN UNMARKED CAR and two WPCs. But it was not Laura they were tending to. Alison was screaming. Frank could hear her as he pulled onto the drive. No words, just screams. He ran into the kitchen.

Alison was holding Laura. Her arms wrapped round her as if protecting her from stray bullets. The two young WPCs were standing there blankly. One was trying to make soothing motions with her hands.

"Alison!" Frank's voice cut through the sound, slicing it, reducing it, silencing it.

"They are going to take her away," said Alison. "They are trying to take her." Her eyes bored blankly into him.

"Alison," he said gently. He licked his lips. He could taste the salt. "They are not trying to take Laura. They want us all to go, together." He held out his hand. "Trust me. It'll be okay," he said. She took the offered hand. He felt the tremors pass from her hand to his. The skin touching. Joined. Close.

THEY PULLED IN outside a nondescript terraced house. They got out. The sun seemed too bright. Alison still held Frank's hand. They walked into the hallway. Miller was waiting for them.

"Afternoon," he nodded. "This is DS Metcalfe. Rosie."

Frank shook hands with her. She had bright kind eyes.

Miller led them into what would have been the sitting room. He sat down. They followed him, sinking into an old sofa. He turned to Laura.

"Rosie is going to ask you a few questions, Laura. Is that okay?"

Laura nodded. A small movement, that rise and fall of her head.

"Why don't you take Alison next door and give her a cup of tea?"

The WPCs led her away. She followed without complaint. Helpless.

Rosie took Laura away. Frank watched their retreating backs.

"We spoke to Lucy Richards," said Miller bluntly. Frank nodded. "Her account tallies with yours. Well done." Miller looked away. "Do you want to listen to Laura's interview?" He indicated the doorway.

Frank nodded. He followed Miller down the hallway into a small room. It was full of cables, televisions and tape recorders. Alison already had her cup of tea. They all sat down.

ROSIE LED LAURA into the interview room. Various stuffed animals lay on the floor. Rosie pointed out the cameras and the microphones. Laura picked up a small pink sheep and sat down. Her mind was blank now. She floated in the warmth of the room. Her limbs had no sense of control. No knowledge of past or future. Only the present. No decisions. No requirements. Just the tall lady smiling kindly at her.

"I'm just going to ask you a few questions."

Laura nodded. She hugged the pink sheep to her chest and drew her legs up under her, making herself smaller.

"Was Kevin Todd your mother's boyfriend?"

"Yes."

"Did he live with you?"

"Yes."

"For how long?"

"Two years."

"When did he leave?"

"Last autumn."

The questions drifted easily towards Laura. Each one she sent back.

"Why did he leave, Laura?"

Laura looked up at the tall lady. She looked into her eyes. She saw only kindness.

"Can I tell you?" asked Laura.

"Yes," replied Rosie. She sat patiently. Her hands relaxed upon her knees.

"I didn't want to upset mummy," said Laura. Her fingers tightened around the pink sheep.

"It's okay," said Rosie. "I know."

"She loved Kevin. He made her happy." Laura's voice was tumbling now. The words tripping against one another. Frank sat beside Miller. They were both very still. Alison sat between the WPCs.

"He came into my room. She was out. He sat on the bed. Told me I was beautiful." Laura didn't raise her eyes. "He reached out and touched my face. Told me it was about time I learnt a few things about life. I said I didn't want to. He told me it would be our secret. Not to tell mummy."

Rosie sat very still. She waited.

"He pressed me down on the bed. Tried to kiss me. I screamed. I screamed." Laura looked up, straight into Rosie's eyes. "I bit him," said Laura. "I kicked and bit and screamed."

"Then what did he do?" asked Rosie. Her voice tinkled like a piano across the room.

"He swore at me. I said I'd tell mum, unless he left for good."

"Did he leave?" asked Rosie.

Laura nodded.

"Yes. The next day."

"Why didn't you tell your mum, Laura?"

"I didn't want to hurt her. I was trying to protect her. She loved him, you see."

And Rosie did see.

Miller looked at Frank and nodded.

"We'll nail the bastard," he said, his voice thick.

"Thank you," said Frank.

"You are very brave." Rosie told Laura.

Alison had gone totally white. She did not move. Only her fingers trembled, like caged birds.

"Alison," said Frank. He crouched in front of her and took her hands. They were cold. "Alison." She did not move. Her eyes were hooded.

They brought her sweet tea, but she did not respond. Only her lips moved. Though they made no sound, Frank could see that the word was *Kevin*.

FRANK WENT HOME with Alison and Laura. There was a lightness now about Laura that he had never known. As if the telling had relieved her. She lay on the floor with her puppy and for the first time Frank saw her smile. He thought that whatever else happened, whatever he had broken, it had to be worth it for that. She had looked up at him after he had come downstairs from putting her mother to bed.

"Frank," she had said.

"Yes?" he had replied.

"Thank you," she had said and had smiled.

HE RANG MARSHA and asked her to come over. She stood on the doorstep and looked up at him.

"Well?" she asked challengingly.

He smiled ruefully at her.

"I broke the plate," he said. "It can be thrown away now."

He drove slowly home. The summer light was dimming. A weariness crept on him and his eyes sagged. He thought of Marsha's last words to him.

"Is it over?" she had asked.

"No." He had shaken his head. "Not yet."

13

THE MONTHS PASSED. Frank fretted.

"Relax," snapped Miller, when Frank rang him for the third time in one day.

But Frank couldn't. It was his case. He wandered around the house, spilling things, moving things, unable to settle.

"Dad!" shouted Annie.

"What?"

"What have you done with the kettle?" Half laughing, half angry, she glared up at him, her eyes slitty.

"Oh Annie." He put out his arms and hugged her. Held her tight against him.

"It'll be okay," said Annie.

"BLOODY HELL!" said Frank slowly as he picked up the morning newspaper. He stood in the hallway, his eyes flashing over the words.

Brookes Investment Management Fund.

Adam Waverley.

Disappeared.

He picked up the phone.

"Miller," said Frank, his voice biting.

"I know," said Miller, his words snapping like fallen twigs. "He's done a runner."

"Had you spoken to him?"

"Yes. He was scared but wouldn't say anything. Had some smarmy top-notch brief. Bugger."

"How *could* you?" said Frank.

"Leave it Frank."

"Miller!"
But the line was dead.

MILLER RANG the following day and apologised. His voice was still hard and the apology stilted.

"It's okay," said Frank, his anger having passed.

"No," growled Miller. "I should have let you know what was happening. It was your case to begin with."

"Thank you," said Frank, aware of what it had cost Miller to say that.

"We spoke to Tom Hutton last week. He collaborated."

"How did you manage that?" asked Frank, remembering that silent phone line.

Miller laughed humourlessly.

"The joy of wimps is that you can bully them," he said. Frank could hear the swagger in his voice.

FRANK WAITED PATIENTLY for the knots to be unravelled. He wrapped his arms around his waist and longed for his wife. But she was far away and Annie seemed only to flit in and out of the house. Frank found himself left all alone with only muted faces for company.

ALISON SAT BLANKLY in the garden. The past that she had tried so hard to subdue had broken out and figures and words rode in shadowy circles around her.

"Did you have a happy childhood?" she'd asked him.

"I wasn't happy until I met you darling," he'd laughed. His head thrown back. His strong jaw lined with stubble glinted golden against the sunlight.

"No really darling," she'd persisted. "Did you?"

"I'm still a child," he'd said, rolling over until his body pressed against hers. And his body beat against hers until all she could see was the golden tinge of the sun on his hair.

"FRANK," said Miller.

"Yes."

"I tracked down Waverley and Hutton, thought you'd like to know how I got on."

Frank nodded and opened the front door wider to allow Miller into the house. The two men sat in the garden. It smelt of summer. Innocence.

"Well," said Frank softly, after Miller hadn't spoken.

"Well," mimicked Miller. "Hutton's completely senile, not a bone of sense came out of him. Waste of bloody time." He peered moodily at his drink.
"And."
Miller smiled twistedly.
"I went to find Waverley but when I got there, only his wife was in."
"Where was he?"
"She wouldn't say. She looked petrified."
"Where do you think he is?"
"I don't think," replied Miller. "I know."
Frank waited and into the silence came the peals of a mobile phone.
"Yes," snapped Miller.
Frank watched him. A slow smile spread across his face. But not a smile of pleasure. Something harder than pleasure. He put his phone in his pocket.
"They have just picked up Waverley and son in Amsterdam. Stupid fool flew straight out to join his son, who'd been hot-footing it round the continent."
"Well done," said Frank. "Well done."

DI MILLER HAD STATIONED his officers around the house. He was sat in an anonymous maroon car. Frank sat beside him. He watched the movement of the men around the house. It made Frank feel slightly sick. The net closing in, the circle tightening. Frank was reminded of an animal in its lair, thinking itself safe. He shook his head, trying to rid himself of the tension that was spreading outwards from his gut.

"You okay?" said Miller, flicking his eyes sideways.

Frank nodded. He looked at Miller's face. He saw a hunter. He watched as Miller's eyes grew sharp, his jaw grew tight. Frank shifted uneasily. Miller muttered into his radio.

Two officers walked up to the front door. The street seemed very quiet. Miller rolled his window down. Frank watched the door open and saw Jo in the doorway. She was wearing a skimpy nightie and her hair was pulled upwards in two pigtails. Everlasting child. Her voice floated across the street, giggling. Innocent. Frank shut his eyes, disgusted.

"I do like a man in uniform." Her voice rose upwards. It flew away from the scene below.

"Kevin. Sure I'll just get him. He's not in trouble is he?" Expecting the answer No. The policemen did not answer.

"Stupid bitch," said Miller violently beside him. Frank flinched. He closed his eyes.

"How can I help you?" Frank opened his eyes and looked up. There he lounged in the doorway. The insolence, the arrogance as transparent as glass. Even from here

Frank could feel the energy pumping off him. Jo hung off his arm, a little girl.

"Mr Todd."

"Yes." That easy smile, those lazy eyes. Frank noticed a young female police officer blush. Watched by wandering eyes, she smiled.

Frank heard the words of arrest. Watched as the handcuffs clamped tightly round his fists. But all through it, Kevin merely stood there, his face open. Jo was crying, her mouth a splash of red.

"Kevin, what's happened?"

"Nothing, darling. It's just a mistake. Misidentity I should think. Don't worry."

And his voice was so *blasé*, his assumption of innocence so strong, that Frank could see even the policemen looked a little puzzled.

Frank watched the police car drive away. But there was no sense of release, of safety. An instinctive unease crept up and wrapped around him. Miller, who had watched the arrest without comment, turned towards Frank.

"I don't trust him. He went too quietly. That always unnerves me. They should struggle, should fight." He chewed his lip, his eyes still on the departing police car. "Well." He tapped his thumbnail on his front tooth, a gesture that Frank had always found repulsive.

Frank shrugged his shoulders. It was too endlessly depressing. He sighed.

"Go home," said Miller, looking at him. "Get drunk." He spoke with the endless sadness of one who has acknowledged too many flaws in his fellow humans.

Frank got out of the car and began to walk along the pavement. The motion of his legs began to soothe him. The simplicity of placing one foot in front of another delighted him. It required no thought, no courage. The plain repetition eased through his weary body. But where he expected to feel pleasure there was none. He tried to examine his feelings of anxiety, but they slipped away like shadows and he could not touch them. There was something unfinished about this case that fluttered around him, haunting him, but he could not grasp it. It eluded him.

He passed two teenagers sharing a cigarette on a bench. They watched him, their faces blank. He sighed. For the lives that had been touched by that golden boy. He let himself into his house and carefully locked the door behind him. Pushing the barely used security chain into place. He leant his back against the door and felt the weakness slither into his legs.

MARSHA SAT BESIDE ALISON in the pretty garden. The flowers had opened fully under the summer sun. Laura played on the grass with the puppy. Marsha watched her run across the grass. Her limbs moving freely now, as if her anguish had reached into her very joints. Alison did not speak. Marsha watched Laura run with the puppy, as it delighted in its own joyfulness, so that they danced, a picture of childhood contentment.

"Shall I make some tea?" asked Marsha.

A slight flexion of the neck. Marsha, taking that as a Yes, retreated to the kitchen.

Alison stared blankly across the garden. But she did not see the flowers, or her daughter. She saw only Kevin. She did not like what she saw.

A technicolour film unfolded before her eyes. A coldness in his eyes as he smiled. A cruelty as he held her at arm's length, playing, dangling, tormenting. She felt the familiar sensation of unease in her gut, but only now could she place it. She looked up.

Marsha walked over, focusing on the tray. She placed it carefully on the ground.

"I knew," said Alison. "I knew."

"Knew what?" replied Marsha, stirring the tea.

"I knew he was bad."

Marsha looked up at her.

"What do you mean?"

"It was always there, all along." Alison kneaded her hands into her lap, trying to force the understanding outwards.

"What, the badness?"

"Yes," said Alison sadly. "Things I accepted as normal that I knew weren't." She turned to Marsha, who handed her a cup. "Why was I so blind?"

"You weren't blind. You were blinded. There is a difference."

"How?" Alison looked at Marsha in confusion.

Marsha sighed.

"He has the ability to make wrong seem right. To disguise and alter your own sense of good and evil. That is why he is so dangerous. He erodes your own senses, till he can control you."

"But why didn't I see that? Why didn't I feel that, as it happened?"

"Because you didn't want to," said Marsha. She peered into her cup. "He represented everything you most wanted. Stability, security, masculinity. He becomes whatever you want him to be. He was perfect. But flawed." Marsha stopped. She remembered his body against hers. Her toyboy. Her sex without strings. "I was just as blind as you were," she said. She swilled her cup and refilled it. "He made me believe that it was okay to still sleep with him, when he was with you. Convinced me our relationship was different to yours, so it wasn't wrong. Of course it was bloody wrong." Marsha punched the ground furiously with her fist.

"What did you not see?" asked Marsha then, half curious, half reluctant.

"Everything," said Alison, "and nothing." She grew silent. The images guttered, steadied, grew strong. A raised fist, a purple bruise. "He hit me," she said, the words blurting into the tranquillity of the garden. "He made me have no faith in my own beliefs, just in his." Her eyes grew wider. The memories fell around her like confetti. "I did everything," she said, "he told me to. Everything. I adored him. Why was I so stupid?"

She shuddered, and the tea slopped over the side of the cup and dripped to the ground like tears.

"You are not stupid."

"But he said."

"See," Marsha snapped. "There. His words. His thoughts."

"He'll always be here," said Alison, looking round.

"No," said Marsha sharply.

"Yes." Alison's voice was soft now, accepting. "All around me. In the wind, his voice. In the walls, the indentation of his face. More alive, more real than in life."

"He's going to go to prison," said Marsha.

"His body, yes, but..." Her voice trailed off.

"No," said Marsha, growing angry now. "You will get through this, Alison. You will. And you will move on and date and get married again and..." She threw her hands into the air.

Alison just shook her head.

"Don't you see Alison. If you give up, he's won."

"But he has won," said Alison bleakly. "He has beaten me."

"No."

"Oh Marsha. You are very kind. But you see I loved him and he betrayed me, destroyed my trust."

"So did Jason. He betrayed you. You managed. You saw other people, you dated."

"But I didn't love him."

"Yes you did, Alison. You did, you married him, you loved him."

"No," she replied obstinately. "I loved Kevin."

Marsha shook her head.

"Don't confuse love with lust Ali. Don't."

"I'm not." She turned snarling towards Marsha. "I know the difference between love and lust and I loved him."

"Why? Why did you love him? He betrayed you, manipulated you, cheated on you, lived off you and finally tried to seduce your daughter, and you *loved* him?"

"Leave me alone. I know what I felt." His hands around her throat and his words tickling her ears. You love me, don't you, don't you. Yes she'd murmured, always. Good. He'd lifted her up, fingers encircling her neck, so that she'd dangled. Say it, he'd said. I love you.

"Ali," pleaded Marsha.

But her pleas were in vain. She watched as Alison wrapped her arms around herself, held herself. No one could touch her, no one could reach her.

MARSHA HAD RUNG FRANK. Her anger had pounded down the phone line making his hand throb.

"She still won't accept it," she'd said, her voice edged with flames.

"Well, it will be hard," he'd said, soothingly.

A snort of irritation.

"Says she doesn't think any of this happened. Says he's not like that. I ask you."

"You forget how strong you are Marsha," Frank had replied.

"And she's not even consistent," Marsha had continued, heedless of Frank's words. "One moment he's the Devil and the next he's misunderstood. *Misunderstood.*" Another snort, though this one tinged with sympathy.

"Marsha, Marsha," he'd said. "You know how convincing he is yourself. Don't be so harsh on her."

She had put the phone down with muttered apologies.

THE NEXT DAY he had walked quietly into town. He turned the corner into the square and, as he did so, he could hear screams. He ran forwards towards a small group of people. In the centre stood Jo, Alison and Marsha. He could see Marsha's mouth opening and closing, but her words were drowned out by the frenzied screams of Jo.

Frank pushed forwards between the three women. Jo's arms were flying around, wings to her words. He grabbed her wrists.

"Stop it!" he snapped sharply.

Jo stopped, her red mouth open, the tip of her tongue protruding, flecks of spit glistening on her chin.

"Accusing us of that!" screamed Marsha into the silence. She stopped and flushed, her head hanging.

The two women like stags waiting to re-engage.

"Right ladies," said Frank, "what's the problem?"

"Who the fuck are you?" asked Jo, recovering her tongue and snapping her arm away from Frank's grasp.

"Frank," said Frank slowly.

"She," Marsha stabbed viciously at the air in front of Jo, "is accusing us of setting Kevin up, out of jealousy."

"Just cos you can't keep a man for more than two bloody minutes!" shrieked Jo, her voice rising high above the ring of onlookers.

"At least I'm not a slapper!" Marsha spat back, her eyes narrow and dark.

Alison said nothing. She stood slightly behind Marsha and to one side, and was seemingly unaware of the chaos around her.

"Kevin wouldn't do a thing like that," said Jo.

Frank looked at her. Her eyes had softened at the mention of his name. Large and brown they looked up at Frank, beseeching him to agree.

"Quite."
"He wouldn't."
"He's nice."
"Handsome."
The voices from the crowd joined in.

ALISON TURNED AND PUSHED her way blindly out of the circle. Her feet stumbling on the cobblestones. Her eyes blurred by confusion. Frank followed her. As he left, the women's voices seemed to pursue him.

"A good man."

He found her standing on the corner by the newsagent. She looked lost. As if unaware of where her feet rested.

"Alison," he said. He handed her a cigarette. "You did the right thing you know," he said.

"Did I?" she asked. "Did I?" She took a long drag on the cigarette and watched the smoke drift away, swirling in the tiny up-currents.

"He's a bad man, Alison. You have only brought his fate upon him. Justice."

"But how do you know everything those girls said is true? Maybe they're lying." The last thread of hope.

"They are not lying." Frank cut the thread. But still she held onto it. A small tatty hope, but a hope.

"Why should I believe you?" she turned on him.

He shrugged his shoulders.

"No one's telling you to believe me. But your daughter? Do you believe your daughter?"

"I don't know." She shook her head helplessly. "I don't know."

Frank watched her. The confusion spiralled outwards from her eyes across her face. He didn't know what to say. Didn't know how to convince her.

"It'll be okay," he said. He stretched out a hand and let his fingers rest lightly upon her shoulder. A feather touch.

"There you are," said Marsha. "Come on." She linked her arm briskly through Alison's and dragged her off. And Frank was reminded of a dandelion clock. Being blown wherever the wind took it.

ALISON FELT AS THOUGH the tiny fragments of control she had once had, had been taken away. She felt as though people were tugging against her as if she were a rag doll, and the seams were beginning to rip. The incident in the town with Jo was only the start.

That evening her old friend Jill Bryant telephoned. Laura answered it.

"Hello Jill. Yes I'm fine. I'll get mummy."

Alison lifted the phone tentatively to her ear. It felt hot and heavy.

"Ali." Jill's voice was as brisk as ever. Her decisive tones cut through Alison's head.

"Hello Jill. How are you?"

"Fine, fine. That wasn't really why I was ringing though."

"No," said Alison, holding the phone with both hands. "I suppose not," she said sadly.

"Look here, Ali. We've been friends a long time haven't we?" She didn't wait for an answer. "I know you very well. Look, about Kevin. I know you thought he was great and all and I'm sorry you felt that bad when he left, but really you can't go round getting people arrested on trumped up charges just for revenge. I really do think you are being a little over the top and vindictive. Don't you, Ali?"

"Um." Alison hung onto the phone wishing it could hold her up, answer for her. But Jill was well away now.

"I mean really, Ali. We all know he's a little well dodgy. But only minor piddly stuff. Just what he's like. Happy go lucky. I really do think you have taken this far enough now. I mean making up things like that. It's a bit disturbing quite frankly. I mean child abuse. That's sick. I mean you've really gone a bit far. Getting a private eye and everything to make it look convincing. Very neat. But really. You've had your fun. Just drop it now, Ali. Really I mean it. Ali?"

But the receiver hung loosely in the empty kitchen and the only reply was the sound of tyres on the driveway. A squeal of rubber on tarmac and then only silence.

ALISON DROVE THROUGH THE DARKNESS. She carried on driving and the roads grew narrower and the hedges taller and eventually she stopped. Everywhere she turned she saw his face, heard his voice. But even her memories were tinged now with sadness, for she had at last truly seen him.

"FRANK."

"What's happened?" asked Frank, his arms prickling with unease at the tone in Miller's voice.

"He got bail. I couldn't get an injunction for Alison and Laura. Probably worth keeping an eye on them."

Miller coughed.

"Will do," said Frank, not letting the cold sweat penetrate his voice.

He pulled up outside Alison's house. It was dark. Her car was missing. He frowned and turned back to his own car. But a sound rang out of the house. He strode quickly to the door. Knocked. Silence.

"Hello," Frank cried out.

A jangling medley of bolts and chain.

"Frank."

Laura stood on the doorstep. Her eyes wide. Her thin body shaking. In her hand she held a knife.

"It's okay," said Frank. "It's me. What's up?"

She shook her head blankly. The blade trembled in her hand.

"Here." He eased the knife out of her grasp and led her inside.

"Where's your mum?" he asked. The warmth of the words bringing life back to her cheeks.

"She's gone out." The words were so small they barely reached Frank.

"What happened?" he asked.

"A car." She stumbled over the words. "A car kept on driving past. Slowing, speeding up. Stopping outside, revving its engine."

"It's okay," said Frank, a coldness inside him. "I'll look after you."

Alison arrived home two hours later. Frank met her at the door, his eyes hard and narrowed.

"Where the hell do you think you've been?" he snapped.

She looked up at him. Her eyes swam, a mass of doubt and fear.

"Sorry," she said. Her face tensing against his anger.

"Oh God. I'm sorry. Come on." They sat down. "It's just you'd left Laura and she was scared."

"I can't do this," said Alison, suddenly. Her hands crashing to the table. "Everyone thinks I'm lying, they think I made it all up."

The next day Alison took Laura shopping.

"We'll have a nice girly day," said Alison. Her voice trembled.

"That would be lovely Mummy," said Laura, watching her mother.

Alison smiled bravely. Wallpaper over a ravine.

They drove to the town and wandered just like any other mother and daughter through the crowded streets.

"This is lovely," said Alison. She held up a pretty top, flowery and girly.

Laura wrinkled her nose up and pulled out a drab coloured top.

"I like this." At least it would cover her up.

"Lovely dear," said Alison, her mind tumbling.

They drove home. The scent of the hedgerows filling the car so that Laura believed for a moment that nothing had happened and it was just another summer's evening, another day. Flat. Boring. She craved boredom. Craved anything but that churning fear that riddled her body and made her feel faint with dread.

They opened the door and stopped. There was something in the house that made them halt. Together without words they moved slowly forwards. Their feet soundless upon the floor.

Alison gasped.

"The pictures." She pointed.

Laura looked.

Where before had hung a pretty painting of a water meadow, there was now an austere portrait of some ancestor that hitherto had resided in the guest bedroom. They walked slowly round the house, neither spoke. Every picture had been moved. None had been damaged and none had been taken. But every single one hung in a different place.

THERE WAS SCREAMING in his ear. The note high and searing. He spun up her drive. He seemed to have slipped back in time, back to the beginning.

Alison was on the floor, rocking.

Laura had wrapped her arms around her, a mother holding a child.

"He's moved the pictures," said Laura, her voice flat.

And Frank remembered the fractured picture in his hall and felt a sickness creep through him.

"WE CAN'T DO ANYTHING," said Miller.

"But it's intimidation," pleaded Frank.

"You can't prove it," said Miller.

"I can," said Frank.

"It's not that bad," said Miller.

But Frank could hear the doubt in Miller's voice.

14

A MONTH OR SO LATER. Frank was sitting in the netherlands of dusk. The sky was tipped with darkness, sorrowfully the sun had sunk and the air was heavy. Frank took a sip of whiskey. He tilted his head back, feeling the liquid roll gently down his throat. The phone rang. He picked it up. The receiver lay lightly in his hand.

"Hello, is that Frank Hargreaves?" said a voice.

"Yes?" said Frank slowly. He slid his glass onto the desk and sat up. His fingers tensed around the phone.

"Who is this please?" he asked, cautious now.

There was silence. The phone seemed to hum.

"My name is Fenella Hand. You spoke to my father a while ago. James Young. About the dogs, our dogs." The voice sank on the last few words, the Australian accent thickening slightly, as if in defence.

"Yes," breathed Frank. Young. Dogs. Kevin.

"My brother called. He heard about the arrest. Kevin's arrest. Said you were in charge. I thought." She stopped, as if in doubt.

"You thought?" prompted Frank. His voice sounded tinny in his ear.

"I wanted," she said, her voice spinning across the continents. "I wanted to tell you." She stopped again.

"Yes?" asked Frank, his voice sharper than he had intended.

"My story," she replied softly. "I wanted to tell you my story."

"Oh," he said, sinking back into his chair, needing the solid feel of its back.

"I never told anyone, except Ed, my brother, you see. I thought perhaps it might help."

"It might," said Frank sorrowfully. He sighed. The sigh travelled miles.

"I'm sorry," said Fenella, backing off. "I shouldn't have bothered you."

"No," said Frank. "Please tell me. Please tell me your story."
"Ok," said Fenella. "I will."

"I WAS SIXTEEN. He was older. Seventeen, I think, or thereabouts. We went to the same school. He walked me home. We chatted. About the future mainly. What we wanted to do. My mum invited him in. What a nice boy, she said, when he left. I smiled. He began to walk me home every day. He was lovely. He listened. He understood." She paused. Outside the sun shone. She was sixteen again. In England Frank put the phone on speaker and placed his head upon the desk. Tired. "We kissed." Fenella's voice filled the room.

The park railings cold against her head. His breath. Hands. Pulsing. His tongue. Not the usual teenage maulings. Gently his lips pressed. Her tongue seeking him out. Crying out, her body strained towards him.

Gently he pushes her back. Holds her against the railings. Leans into her. His body pressed against hers. She gasps. He pulls her hair back. She does not feel pain. Laughing he steps away. She moans.

"I became obsessed. He filled my head. There was something so strong about him. Magnetic, maybe."

"What happened?" asked Frank, his voice drained.

"He came to school one day with a key. His friend's flat. He said we could go there after school. To chat."

The door slams behind them. The air is cold. His hands on her face. She groans. Their tongues fuse. He pushes her down on the bed. His hands on her shoulders. His hand inside her skirt. She wriggles. A hand on her chest. The other pulls his trousers down. He leans against her. Wait, she says, her breath in gasps now. Stop. Why? His tongue strokes her lips. We can't. Her brain fights her body. He leans into her. His breath is hot. Scared are we? he taunts. He traps her legs. Please, she begs, please don't. Tears on her eyelids. Fine, he rolls away. Please don't be cross, she scrambles towards him. You're a kid, he snaps. He pushes her roughly. She bangs her head. He gets up. *Kevin* she cries out. The flat door slams.

"I went home. Crying. Told my mother he had split up with me. But he's such a nice boy, she told me. What did you do? Only my father looked pleased. Told me everything would be okay. Three days later we found the dogs."

"I'm sorry," said Frank in England. "I'm so sorry."

"It's okay," said Fenella. In Australia the sun was bright. "I'm okay now," she said. Quietly she put the phone down.

"Goodbye," said Frank to the dead phone.

He sat for a long time in the sparsely lit room.

AT SCHOOL LAURA SITS ALONE in the corner of the yard. She draws her legs up under her and perches on the wall in the corner. Alone she shuts her eyes tightly and longs for the night, when she may sleep and not dream.

"Oi!"

She opens her eyes. Below her stand three boys. They look up at her, their eyes bright, flashing.

"Think you're smart do you?" they chant. Their voices rise like steam, hot air, the words mingle with the air and drift around her, through her. She looks away.

"Oi! We're talking to you!" The louder words do not make more sound, they simply rise quicker, pass by quicker.

"Tease! That's what you are! That's what you did wasn't it? Teased him!" The word hummed round her, a small bird.

"My mum said he ain't no kiddy fiddler, and you're just a liar. Liar. Don't think you'll get away with it!" The words burned now. Their heat touches her cold cheeks, brand her, mark her. Liar. Tease. She hugged her knees.

"We want a bit of you!"

She looked down. The boys were laughing. Their mouths pulled back, the winter sun glinting off their teeth. They thrust their hips towards her. Rhythmically. She bit her tongue. The taste of blood brought clarity and the pain lifted her above their eyes and transported her far away.

Below she heard a teacher bellow. Felt the air move as he swung his arms in fury. Heard the scuttling feet on the concrete. The silence.

"Laura," said Mr Jems.

She looked down.

"Why don't you come down off there and come and have a cup of tea?"

She slid off the wall and followed him inside the main building.

The tea was hot. The smell of the sugar rose off the surface. He pushed her a plate of biscuits. She ignored him, concentrating on her tea. She looked out of the window. The pigeons were clustering around the drainpipes. She watched them fight and jostle for a place. She watched their beaks open and close as they chattered to one another. She wondered what they were saying.

"Laura."

The kindness of his voice drew her back into the room. Harshness she could filter out, but kindness no. Kindness penetrated her defences and left her vulnerable and cold.

"Are you okay?" he asked smiling at her.

She stared back at him. Answers she knew she could not release. Stifled by them she simply nodded blankly.

"I thought maybe you should take next week off," he continued. "The trial starts next week doesn't it?"

She nodded again.

"How about some time off?" he repeated.

She nodded. It was simpler than speech. Words seemed too loaded now, too heavy with guilt and responsibility. She looked away. She felt his sigh ruffle the air.

IN NOTTINGHAM Sam Johnson very gently replaced the telephone on its cradle. He looked out of the window. Autumn had crept up, surprising him. The leaves were twirling softly to the ground. He leant against the glass. The cold from outside seeped through it and into his skin. He stretched his hands in front of him. The bones cut through the skin, giving the impression of a skeleton emerging from its wrapping. The words drifted through his head, producing a musical accompaniment so that they danced with an unorthodox gaiety.

"I'm afraid Effie Todd passed away in the early hours of this morning."

Passed away. He looked upwards. But the sky seemed too grey to accommodate her. He moved his eyes downwards again and let them rest upon the garden. The flowers were settling down to sleep. He envied them, with a pain more akin to anger than to grief. Wished that he too could sleep and let the months, seasons, years swirl past him, without touching.

He pushed himself off the window and turned towards the stairs. Upstairs he sat on his bed and reached under it. He fished out an old shoebox. He placed it on his lap and for a long time sat without movement. Passed away. The words danced lightly through his mind. He felt no grief, for in his mind she had died the day she had been placed in that nursing home. A halfway house before death. A discreet place to rot silently. Anger made him flush. He lifted the lid of his shoebox and looked inside.

It was fairly empty. He peered at the contents for a while, before reaching surely inside. He pulled out one photograph. It was black and white and had been taken about thirty years ago. He looked at it, though he knew its contents well. He saw himself, mid-thirties, smiling, eyes narrowed against the sun, his arm flung casually over Effie's shoulder. She was smiling. Her face seemed to sparkle at him across the years. That was Effie, not some cold body in a nursing home. He padded back downstairs carrying his photo. He pinned it carefully in the kitchen. Pride of place. He stood back examining it.

"I'm sorry, Effie," he said.

He picked up the phone again.

FRANK LAY HALF ASLEEP, lounging back in his office chair. It was mid morning. He was meant to be reading the newspaper but had found the endless words too tiring to contemplate and had given up. He was existing in that unpleasant limbo that he recognised from old. The vacuum of time between the arrest and the trial. He occupied his days by taking on small surveillance jobs, but his mind drifted constantly to Alison and to Kevin. Miller had informed him that all was well and the case looked to be successful, but still there was the waiting to contend with. So Frank snoozed gently. The rise and fall of his breathing making the paper follow his chest, fluttering slightly.

The phone rang. The noise dragged him from his half-sleep and he sat up slowly, hand groping across the desk towards the phone.

"Hello?" He yawned.

"Mr Hargreaves, this is Sam Johnson." The voice seemed resigned.

"Sam Johnson?" Frank sat bolt upright, the paper slithering forgotten to the floor, adrenaline pulsed. "From Nottingham?"

"Yes." A sadness underlining the resignation. "I wondered if you could come and see me. I would like to talk to you."

FRANK DROVE QUICKLY, as though the car was picking up on his own bubbling excitement. The roads, for once accommodating, were clear. Frank sped swiftly towards the city. He followed the route into the suburb, noticing as Sam Johnson had earlier the tumbling leaves. Frank liked autumn. He regarded it as cleansing, a chance for a new start, a new beginning. He liked watching the plants curl up, waiting for sleep to take them. He thought they deserved their rest after a summer of growing and pleasing people. He turned down Sam Johnson's road and braked roughly. He eased his car into a space and jumped out.

Sam Johnson must have been watching for him, for the door swung open as he lifted his hand towards the knocker. Sam did not greet him, he simply turned away and retreated down the corridor towards the kitchen. Frank followed, bouncing slightly on the balls of his feet. He entered the kitchen. Sam was already attending to the kettle, as if regretting his invitation. Frank waited patiently. He watched Sam's hands as he ground the coffee beans. They shook slightly. With great precision and concentration he poured the coffee and placed one mug in front of Frank. He sat down. He stared down at the table. Traced the grain with his nail. Newly bitten, noted Frank. His senses so acute that he could feel the slight breeze from the crack by the window. The smell curled round him, drawing him downwards, distracting him. He watched the movement of Sam's finger, watched as it stilled and watched as Sam lifted his head and looked deep into his eyes.

"Effie Todd died this morning," he said.

"I'm sorry," said Frank.

There was silence again and Sam returned his attention to the grain of the wood. Frank drank his coffee, enjoying the sharp taste of the fresh bean.

"I loved her," said Sam.

Frank looked at him. His eyes were so clear, his expression of love so simple.

"I loved her for years, years," Sam repeated, a half smile twisting his face. "That's why I wouldn't tell you," he said, grappling with the words. "Because I promised. I promised her I wouldn't." He turned away, but Frank could still see his fingers twisting. He turned back to Frank and dropped his hands by his sides. "But she's dead now. Dead. The promise is discharged."

"What promise?" asked Frank, the words barely touching him.

Sam sat down. He sighed. A breath that seemed to expel the years that had passed, so that suddenly he was young again, filled with hope and future.

"My sister Ellie was married to Martin Richards. She had two children, Mark and Lucy." His eyes were flat. "She died not long after giving birth to Lucy. Complications they said. I became Effie's lover not long after my sister died. Her husband died a few years later."

His voice curled round Frank, drawing him into the past. The present was forgotten.

"I was Uncle Sam to Mark and to Kevin. I was happy." He looked up at Frank and the past danced between them. "Martin rang me one afternoon and asked me to come round. His voice was faint, trembling. I went as quickly as I could."

THE HOUSE WAS VERY QUIET when he arrived, as if a blanket had been thrown over it, hiding it from the world. Sam ran up to the front door. It stood open. He went inside. In the hallway the phone hung from the wall, off the hook. A dark stain encircled the receiver. Worried now, Sam ran to the kitchen. Martin was sitting at the table, his head in his hands. When he lifted his head to look at him, Sam could see two handprints of blood.

"What happened?" asked Sam, stumbling forwards.

But Martin drew back.

"Don't touch me," he hissed.

Martin stood up and walked out of the back door down the garden. Sam followed a little distance behind. At the shed door, Martin stood back. Reluctantly Sam walked up to the door and opened it. He gagged, hand to his mouth, retching. In the centre of the hut was a chair and bound to the chair was a boy. But he had no face. And the only sound was Sam's own breath. The sweet, sickly smell of blood rose up and overwhelmed him.

"JESUS," exclaimed Frank.

Sam looked at him and twitched.

"It was barbaric," he said. "I asked him why he'd done it, but when I heard I almost wished I hadn't." He ran his hands down his face.

"He told you about Lucy, then?" asked Frank.

Sam nodded.

"He kept on saying 'Sister, sister.'"

"What did you do?"

"I called Effie and Adam and Tom's parents."

"Hutton and Waverley."

"Yes," nodded Sam. He shook his head. "What sickens me now is the fact that we virtually ignored Lucy. As if this monstrosity wiped out the first. The three parents turned up. We dragged Lucy out of her room and made her tell them, the parents, what their sons had done to her. Then we showed them Mark." Sam's voice had hardened now. "Hutton was one of the senior policemen in the area. Detective chief inspector. Waverley was a magistrate. They were more concerned about their own reputation than with the meaning of justice. Law and order. They seemed to regard it as an exercise in public relations. They stood there. Just feet away from the body discussing how to cover the incident up. Effie was sick. She stood there quivering, eyes wide open. Horrified, half-crazed by grief at what her son had done. While these two men just carried on, a normal day."

"What did they do?" asked Frank.

"The practicality of it still repulses me," said Sam.

"What did they do?" asked Frank again.

"Garrets," said Waverley, clicking his knuckles.

"The waste land?" queried Hutton.

"Yes," Waverley nodded.

"Perfect," said Hutton. "We need some plastic."

"They were so prosaic," said Sam.

Frank watched a tear roll down his cheek.

"They wrapped him in plastic, put him in the car and drove him to the old waste land."

"Then?" asked Frank.

"Hutton made sure the official procedure was followed. We reported him missing. He had a young PC sent round after a few days. Wet behind the ears. Poked around in Mark's room, but that was it."

"They never checked anywhere else?" asked Frank.

"Why would they? We said he'd run away." Sam shrugged his shoulders. "It's all they ever do check, the bedroom."

"Then what?" asked Frank.

"We buried him."

Frank stared at Sam.

"But what else could we have done?" Sam spread his hands towards Frank.

"Told the truth," said Frank.

"I wanted to," said Sam. "I did. But I promised Effie I wouldn't. And I couldn't have put Martin in jail. The man my sister loved."

"He might have got off," said Frank. Anger dripped slowly through him. A good man, a weak man. "And what of Lucy?"

Sam shifted in his chair. He flashed an uneasy glance at Frank.

"We just ignored her," he said finally, full of shame. "We didn't know what to do," he said, as Frank's mouth opened in anger. "I know we did wrong, but..."

Frank shrugged his shoulders. In his mouth, only a taste of failure and sadness.

"This investigation has been handed over to the police," he said. "I trust you will not object to talking to them as well." His tone was light, edged with brutality. "A chance to right the wrongs of the past, you might say."

"Of course," said Sam. "Of course I will talk to them."

"Good," said Frank coldly. "Where's the waste land?"

Sam told him meekly.

FRANK STOOD IN THE CENTRE of the waste land. Above him, invisible birds sang mournfully. At his feet lay a small collection of freshly picked flowers.

"Hello Mark," said Frank.

15

ON THE OPENING DAY of the trial Alison cooked Laura pancakes for breakfast. Alison watched the milk, eggs and flour mingle and wondered if so small a gesture would go any way towards assuaging the destruction she had caused her daughter. They did not mention the trial, not once through the whole day. They revolved around one another, like orbiting planets. Not speaking, not touching, but each constantly aware of the other's presence.

In the evening Laura picked up the telephone and spoke to Frank.

"What happened?" she asked, dispensing with formalities.

"Not much," said Frank. "Would you like me to come over?"

"Please," said Laura, unable to cope with her mother alone.

Frank arrived with newspapers.

"Don't show her," snapped Alison, as they spilled across the table, their black letters blaring strongly under the kitchen light.

"Let me see," said Laura.

"No!" shouted Alison grabbing her daughter harshly by the arm.

"Let go of me!" cried Laura, twisting violently.

"I'm trying to protect you," said Alison.

"Well you already failed in that."

Laura's words fell heavily. Alison dropped her arm as if scalded and turned away. Frank could see the tremors spreading along her shoulders and touched her gently on the arm.

Laura sat down, carefully selected the first newspaper and began to read.

"Why did you bring them?" said Alison. The shivers along her shoulders leaked into her voice and the words shook.

"I thought it was better she knew what was going on," replied Frank, frowning, "than leaving it to her imagination."

"Oh," said Alison. She sagged softly into a chair and yanked a paper at random from the pile.

LOCAL MAN IN CHILD ABUSE CASE

Alison tried to look away. But there was a picture underneath the headline. Kevin. Sparkling even through the grimy newsprint his eyes seemed to rest upon her. His hair touched his shoulders and his mouth laughed. And he was there. Leaning against the wall. The sound of his laughter dripping down her back. Aroused. She felt a flush spread down her body into her groin. His hands. His touch. His smell.

She looked up. Laura was calmly reading her way through the papers. After she finished each one she folded it carefully and placed it on the floor beside her. Alison watched her daughter. Saw the tightening of concentration around the corners of her eyes. Saw her mouth hard. A straight line stretched across her face. Saw the curl of hair round her fingers where her hand rested on the side of her head.

"What have I done?" Alison turned to Frank. Her eyes slipping into him, seeking comfort.

"How were you to know?" he replied. His words wrapping round her.

"I should have known."

He shrugged his shoulders and shook his head, unable to reassure her.

"I should have read the signs." Alison put her head in her hands. Her breath felt hot against her skin.

"Mum," said Laura. Her voice cut. "How could you have known? Look." She waved the paper at her mother. Her gestures sharp and precise. "All these people believed him. Some still do." She took her mother's hand in hers. A reversal of maternal protection. "It'll be okay," said Laura. She squeezed her mother's hand in her own and did not let go.

Frank looked out of the window.

"Just think," he said, turning towards them. "If you hadn't wanted to know the truth, he would still be out there, walking freely. And he's not. He's in court. You did that. Be proud."

LAURA FELT THE DAYS PASS as though she and her mother were in a boat. They knew the land was close but did not know where it was, and each day was spent scanning the flat horizon for some shape or sign that would show them that land was nearby.

They seemed to camp in their own house. Barely moving, as if conserving their energy, or keeping very still, like wild animals in the darkness. Frank came every day after court and spoke to them. They came to long for the sound of his wheels on the gravel. His presence cutting through their unspoken tangle of apologies and reassurances. And finally the trial drew to a close, and they waited, growing stiller and stiller, so that soon even the dust would settle on them undisturbed.

The light on the final day of the trial was flat. Shapes seemed to have no depth. Objects that had hitherto been solid, stood as cardboard cut-outs, throwing no shadows upon the dust. As if their shadows had been absorbed into the air, sucked up and flattened. Above them the sky hummed.

They listened to cars on the lane. Until the noise drifted away leaving only silence and the flat sky above them. The sky grew darker. Not wanting to move they did not switch the lights on. Greyness crept from the corners in tendrils across the floor, absorbing the light.

An engine on the lane. A crisp slam of a door. Footsteps in the hall. Still they did not move.

"Ten years!" shouted Frank. "Ten years!" He hit the light switch and in time with his words the room burst into light and the greyness fled away, defeated.

Their eyes quivering as if in doubt.

"We did it," said Frank. His hair stood upright, his trousers crumpled. A small child. "We got him. Ten years. Ten years as the instigator. Adam and Tom got five each and Waverley got three. You did that. You."

16

Laura walked along the cliff top. The spray left a trail of salt on her lips. She ran her tongue over them, feeling them crackle, dried out by the wind. Her feet trod firmly along the narrow path. They moved with ease now, at home. Carefully she navigated the narrowest part of the path: it no longer made her heart race. She turned left away from the cliff and began to cut upwards through the gorse bushes before emerging onto the narrow lane that led to the village. Grass had pushed its way through the tarmac down the centre. She stopped and wondered at the fragile wind-bent strands of flickering green that had burst through the tarmac.

The hill sloped sharply down to the village. A cluster of houses clinging to the rock, the wind shaping them, even in the summer. She pushed open the shop door. The old bell jangled. No one was inside. Laura stopped. The stillness of the air startling after the force of the wind outside. Her hair flopped in tendrils round her face. From the back of the shop a door creaked open. Alistair appeared. One hand pushing his glasses back onto the bridge of his nose, the other clasped round a small girl. His sister.

Laura flinched at the sight of the small child. She averted her eyes and swallowed the acid that had risen through her throat.

"Hi Laura," said Alistair. Ineffectively trying to bump the child higher up his hip.

"Hi," said Laura, her eyes fixed on the wall behind his head.

"Lawlaw," gurgled the child. It detached one arm from its brother's neck and stretched out a podgy hand.

"She likes you," said Alistair.

"Um." Laura scuffed at the floor with her shoe.

"What did you want?" asked Alistair. The child giggled, stretching her hands towards the brightly packaged sweets. "No Alice. No!"

But Laura could not remember what she wanted.

THEY HAD MOVED to Scotland six months after the trial. Laura remembered her mother packing frantically. Crashing between excitement and despair. Laura had not cared about leaving. People had nudged their friends in the street on seeing her. The children at her school had followed her chanting until she had ceased to go and had simply lain in bed watching the patterns of light on her ceiling.

No one here looked at them and saw Kevin in their eyes. Here they were free of him, almost. Laura no longer heard his voice on the wind, nor his footstep with every creaking door. Her mother cooked and cleaned and worked part time for a solicitor in a nearby town. As if nothing had happened, nothing had changed. But at night Laura dreamt of children. They were almost always blonde. These children of her dreams would lie spreadeagled on mown lawns. As she woke sweating in the dawn she could still smell the scent of freshly mown grass. They wore pretty dresses and they screamed. In her dreams they squealed like pigs. Their fear was tangible. And their faces would be streaked with tear stains, though she never saw them cry. And what hurt her most, as she woke shaking, was that throughout the dream she could never lift a finger to save them, but would stroll past their pain and their fingers would scrabble at her legs only to be pulled back by strong, tanned hands. And always at the end there would be silence as they ceased to fight and a resignation would creep upwards and encircle her. Then she would wake bolt upright.

"LAURA?" ASKED ALISTAIR, kindly. "Are you alright?"

She looked up.

"Alistair!" A strong voice from the house carried into the shop.

"Sorry," he said, flushing. The door slammed behind him.

Laura breathed. Her head cleared. Her shopping list surfaced. Milk, bread, something for supper.

Alison had got into the habit of sending Laura to do the shopping. At first she had refused, seeing men's eyes in every brick, stone, gorse bush that lay in the way. But gradually the eyes were fading. Now she almost liked going to the little shop. Unchallenging, undemanding. She felt proud of herself, proud of her own strength and courage.

The door swung open again. Alistair reappeared, minus the child.

"Sorry," he said, pushing his hair back off his face.

They collected the shopping together and he packed it for her into the small rucksack she carried.

"Thank you," she said, watching his hands move, clasp and release. Watching the tendons flex under the skin.

"Laura."

She looked at him. A faint brushstroke of pink lay along his cheekbones.

"There's a dance, tonight, in town. I wondered if you wanted to go."

He looked away. Her stomach churned. The smell of men filled her nose, making her want to retch and run. She breathed deeply, pushing her feet into the earth.

"That would be nice," she replied. Though to her own ears the words sounded like lies.

"Great." His face broke into a puppy-dog smile. "I'll pick you up at eight."

She smiled and left the shop.

SHE RAN BACK along the cliff path towards the little cottage, perched on the cliff a mile out of the village. Laura pushed open the wonky gate that led into the garden and then pushed hard against the front door that had warped and always caught against the flagstones.

Some compulsion to tell her mother, which she did not understand, hit her.

"I'm going to the dance with Alistair," she said.

"Oh darling." Alison stood up. A year had left her skinny and wrinkled, as though her skin was too large for her body. But her eyes danced now. They were light. "How exciting." She held her daughter. The tremors she felt through her hands, she misread as excitement. "Let's find you an outfit, shall we?"

She took her by the hand and led her upstairs. Laura's bedroom faced inland. Out of the window all you could see was an endless vista of the tiny yellow flowers from the gorse bushes. They seemed very bright against the greyness of the sky.

Laura sat on the bed. Her mother rifled through the rails, making small noises of delight or disillusionment.

"Here," said Alison, passing Laura a red dress. "Try this."

Laura stared at it in horror. Such a small piece of material. *You asked for it*, echoed the voices in her head.

"Come on darling." The excitement in her mother's voice was palpable. Reluctantly Laura pulled off her jeans and jumper and yanked the dress over her head.

"Lovely!" Alison clapped her hands in delight.

Laura looked into the mirror.

She saw a tall girl. Long brown hair. Long legs. Short red dress. And sad eyes. And she felt only tiredness.

"It's lovely Mummy," she said blankly.

ALISTAIR DROVE TOO FAST. Laura felt the wheels slip across the road and a flush of panic thudded through her. She held onto her seatbelt. The dress had ridden up her thighs. She stared at her knees. They looked so bare.

"Here we are." Alistair braked sharply and manoeuvred into a small space. He grinned. "Come on." He bounded out. Laura felt cold. Very slowly she opened the door and slid her legs around. She stood up. The dress dropped back into place, just skimming her knees. She breathed. The thump of music from inside billowed out into the car park. She could hear the deep throaty laughter of young men. She shivered.

"Let's go." Alistair took her hand and hurried towards the door. Laura's feet dragged reluctantly, her steps unsure, her feet shaky in their tottery heels. The sound hit her as they entered. The flashing wall of music and writhing bodies loomed out at her. She recoiled.

"Great!" shouted Alistair. His hand felt hot, its fingers curled tightly around her own. Devoid of will she followed him. The bodies hemmed her in. Their smell touched her.

"Here." Alistair pressed a bottle into her hand. Inside the bottle sloshed a bright blue liquid. She put it to her lips: it tasted of summer. Sweet, sickly.

They were in the crowd now. Jostling figures. The sensation of bare skin against her own. Alistair was dancing wildly, throwing his arms above his head. She shuffled reluctantly from side to side.

Behind her someone wrapped their arms around her waist and fitted their body into hers. She tensed. Clamping her teeth. She swallowed. Fighting to retain control.

"Oi!" Alistair shoved the man. She felt his arms disengage and the warmth of his body disappear. "You ok?" cried Alistair. She nodded.

A boy and girl entwined stood very still among the seething figures. Laura watched as they curled their heads together, watched the fusion, meeting of lips and tongues. The girl pulled back. Her eyes shone.

A face loomed in front of her. A man. Heavy forehead. Dark eyes. His smell enfolded her.

"Give us a kiss, darling." The face swayed drunkenly.

Laura ran. It seemed that the crowd rolled back, sensing her shame. She leant against the wall and looked up. Above, the stars slept. Twinkling dully they hung. She swallowed down the fear. Wished she could join in. Wished she were someone else, somewhere else. Something else. A star.

"Laura?"

Alistair seemed so solid compared to the stars. His shoulders stretched broadly in front of her, but she did not feel hemmed in. His voice fluttered gently in her ears. Her name.

"Come here." He held his arms out wide. Like a father should.

She stepped forwards. Stepped towards a man, and stepped into his embrace. His arms folded round her like wings, nestling down. She laid her head upon his chest and softly he stroked her hair. She breathed. Slowly she lifted her head. His eyes smiled softly down. She reached up. Their lips met. She paused, half waiting for a well of nausea, but none came. This was not harsh, nor angry. This was soft and gentle and good. She strained upwards towards him, something she did not understand driving her onwards. They hung to each other and then finally pulled apart.

"Oh," she said in soft awe. "Oh."

AFTER HER DAUGHTER had left the house Alison paced. She held the piece of paper in her hands. The one that Frank had sent her. She read his note again. *I'm not sure this is a good idea, but...here you are.* She turned it over. There was a phone number and a name. Kathy.

The trial and conviction had brought Alison release. But floating on the edges of her mind, ever present, had been still the question *Why*. She had the answers in terms of cause and effect. She still did not know *why*.

"He's evil." Frank had groaned down the phone.

"How do you know?" Alison had stamped her foot. "And actually Frank I always meant to ask you, when did you first know?"

"Know?"

"About Kevin."

"Marsha told me she caught him kissing her fourteen-year-old niece. That was when I knew."

"Oh."

And she had rung Marsha.

"Just let it rest now Ali." Marsha had said, her voice filling the small cottage. "It's over."

She had tried. She had let day slip into night, she had let sleep drift over her, numbing her. She had remembered how to laugh and how to cry. She had, though she had as yet not told Laura, started seeing a man. A nice man. She hoped. But still the question appeared. In her bath the previous night, the bubbles had formed a question mark, or so she told herself. The question loitered, catching her as she ran into the village shop, as she typed a letter, as she looked at the sea. It was politer than before. No longer did it feast off her. It waited patiently. But like a drip of water it persevered.

She dragged the small stool over to the window and sat down. The last of the evening light tiptoed across the water. The waves moved monotonously. She picked up the phone in one hand and watched as the other danced over the numbers, like a pianist over a keyboard.

"Hello."

She stared at the phone in wonder that it spoke.

"Hello," she said slowly, doubtingly. "Is that Kathy Mace?"

"Yes," said the voice hesitantly.

"My name," said Alison clearly, as if to a child, "is Alison Mannings."

A gasp. Of shock, disgust.

"I'm sorry," said Alison. "You know who I am then?" A lingering question.

"Yes," said Kathy. The word a breath. "I do."

"I just wanted." Alison stopped, she cradled the telephone and leant her head on the window pane. "I wanted to talk to you about Kevin."

"Why?" asked Kathy. The tension quivered down the phone line.

"I wanted to understand," said Alison. "Understand why. I'm sorry."

"No," said Kathy. But to what Alison did not know.

"Sorry," said Alison again, as if the mere word could wipe out the past, the future, the blood.

"No it's okay," said Kathy. A touch of sadness glowed, went out. "What did you want to know?"

"I just wondered if anything happened, you know, when he was young. Whether there was a reason for what he did, or whether it was simply..."

In the silence, the unspoken word. Stretched out between them, it pushed them apart, pulled them together.

"Our father," said Kathy. Her voiced lurched. "He was violent."

Alison slumped downwards. Her muscles sagging, flapping against her bones.

"I'm sorry," she said. Empty words.

"He used to hit Kevin." The sound of a fist. The crunch of bone. The tear of flesh. Blood. "It doesn't excuse what Kevin did but it does explain it. I think." She began to sob. The sound reached Alison and fled until it mingled with the sounds of the waves. "He was my brother," she said. "My brother. And I adored him. Loved him. But he took no notice of me. Couldn't bear families. I think he wanted to rip them apart, deprive others of what he couldn't have." Her words slipped into her tears and the tears into the waves and in the end all that Alison could hear were the waves.

She put the phone down. She went to the back door. She let herself out into the darkness. The taste of salt on the air touched her lips. Above, the moon leapt out. It tinged the tops of the waves. Alison walked steadily to the cliff. She stood on the edge and looked down. Then she tilted her head back and looked up. Above her the stars remained unchanged. Unconcerned they formed their patterns and littered the sky in pictures.

Alison turned. She walked back to the house. Her footsteps fell more firmly upon the ground and the ground in turn felt more solid beneath her feet. The cottage walls stood up proudly and the lights burned cheerfully. And where before everything had seemed to liquefy and blend, now everything stood out. Every surface, every colour. A brick. A wall. A colour. A man. Perhaps not evil. Perhaps evil. But perhaps half pushed, half tempted into the places where evil lies. And though, as Kathy had said, it was no excuse, it was perhaps an explanation, a reason, an answer.

Suddenly weary she stumbled on the stairs. Her bed beckoned. The duvet closed round her, holding her, comforting her. As sleep rushed up, she thought she heard the sound of laughing children.

THE NEXT DAY BROUGHT RAIN. Laura sat at the open window and let the raindrops touch her, as though they could wash her clean, strip her bare, reveal her. She touched her lips. They tingled as if in memory. She smiled hugging herself in delight. Downstairs the door slammed. She heard sounds of greeting. Josie. She padded down the stairs. Her mother and Josie sat on the floor, their voices twittering. Between them on the carpet lay Abby. Two years old with blonde hair and a little pink dress. Laura stopped on the threshold. She kept her eyes glued on the child and began to step carefully forwards. She knelt down.

"May I?" she said arms outstretched towards the small gurgling creature.

Josie nodded. Alison stilled, her eyes upon her daughter.

Hardly breathing Laura put her hands around the small child. Carefully she lifted it. It hung grinning in her hands. Gently Laura bent her arms until the child rested against her chest. She held it. It smelt sweet.

Alison stared at her daughter holding the small child. Tears of something, maybe release, spilled down her face. Spreading across Laura's face was a smile.

17

Even from Australia, her voice reached him strongly.
"Be careful Ed," said Fenella.
"Don't worry, sis," replied Edward. "Anyway, no one will care."

The cell was sparsely furnished. There was a bed. On the bed lay a man. He stared moodily at the ceiling. Unfair, he thought, I did nothing wrong. Grumpily he kicked out. A small chunk of plaster fell to the floor. The dust settled. The man watched the sunlight creep across the ceiling. A spider scuttled away.

In the corridor outside, footsteps echoed. Their tread sure and unyielding. The prisoner on the bed took no notice. He had grown used to the sound of footsteps, the mindless stamp of the warders who roamed the corridor. They were simply a fact. As were the other inmates, who curled their lips at him and called him scum. He did not know why. He was innocent. He was set up. Those girls had loved it. Lucy had asked to play with them. Young teens in short skirts. Fresh flesh. Their dimpled mothers. Who would you choose?

The spider had stopped. A fly wriggled in its web. The prisoner watched in disgust as the spider advanced upon the fly. He shut his eyes. He could almost hear the scrunch of small fly bones. He shuddered.

The footsteps had stopped. The handle creaked. The door swung open. The prisoner sat up.

"Hello," he said.

"Hello," said the warder. He smiled.

The prisoner saw a flash of a knife. A warning. He frowned.

"What's up mate?" He licked his lips. Sweat popped along his brow.

The warder drew out a length of rope. He advanced. The knife held steadily in front of him. Its tip pointed at the man's throat.

"Hey!" said the man.

The warder saw the fear pulse through the prisoner's eyes and smiled.

He wound the rope around the prisoner's neck, his fingers steady. His eyes rested upon the man. Carefully he looped the rope over the metal bars that fastened to the window.

Holding the rope, he dragged a chair over.

"Get up." His voice flat.

The prisoner in front of him shook. The warder placed the point of the knife against the man's throat.

"I said get up."

The man got up. He stood on the chair. A trickle of fluid ran down his leg and seeped onto the chair, staining it.

Carefully the warder adjusted the rope. He stepped back. He smiled.

He kicked the chair away.

The prisoner swung. His arms and legs lashed furiously. One fist hit the window and the glass cracked. The sunlight beat through the cracked glass and dispersed. Like a kaleidoscope.

"Goodbye Kevin," said Edward Young softly. He replaced his warder's cap and shut the door gently behind him.

But Kevin did not reply.

Thanks

Loads of thanks to Martyn and Charles.
They know why.
And to my editors Peter Brookesmith and Lesley Riley,
who turned my ramblings into a coherent novel.
And of course to my family for putting up with me.

Printed in the United Kingdom
by Lightning Source UK Ltd.
129305UK00001B/57/P